LAST MAN STANDING

DI SARA RAMSEY
BOOK TWENTY-FIVE

❧

M A COMLEY

For Mum, you never let me down, thank you for giving me the tools and the backing to begin this incredible journey. Thank you for always believing in me.

I miss you every minute of every day; you truly were a Mum in a million. My heart, my soul.

ACKNOWLEDGMENTS

Special thanks as always go to @studioenp for their superb cover design expertise.

My heartfelt thanks go to my wonderful editor Emmy, and my proofreaders Joseph and Barbara for spotting all the lingering nits.

Thank you also to my amazing ARC Group who help to keep me sane during this process.

To Mary, gone, but never forgotten. I hope you found the peace you were searching for my dear friend. I miss you each and every day.

ALSO BY M A COMLEY

PROLOGUE

*R*everend Paul Gains took a final look outside the church door to see if the weather had improved in the last few minutes since he'd waved off the final choir member. It hadn't. If anything, the rain was now coming down in biblical proportions. He shook his head, aware of what the damage to the area was likely to be over the coming days. It didn't take that much to declare Hereford a flood zone, especially with the amount of rain they'd had to put up with over the last couple of hours.

"I've never known a December like it, Vicar, have you?" Mrs Tinder crept up behind him, scaring the crap out of him.

His hand automatically covered his chest. "My goodness, I'd forgotten you were out back, Mrs Tinder. Thought I was the last one here."

"Oh, no, I'm so sorry. My Arthur had a nickname for me. I'm not sure if it's appropriate to tell you what it was or not, given our surroundings."

Paul inclined his head, and his brow knitted. "Ooo, you have me more than a little intrigued. Go on, you'll have to tell me now, dear lady."

1

"Well, before he passed away, I had a habit of appearing behind him when he least expected it—his fault entirely, because, more often than not, the foolish man refused to wear the hearing aid he was given."

"Ah, I see. So, what nickname did he give you then?" He racked his brains but couldn't for the life of him come up with anything that he would have regarded as offensive during their conversation.

Mrs Tinder bowed her head and mumbled something he had trouble understanding because of the lousy conditions outside, battering at the large wooden door to the house of worship. "Creeping Jesus. Can you believe the audacity of the man? How disrespectful using the name of our Lord like that."

Having a sense of humour was always at the top of his agenda; Paul wasn't your average run-of-the-mill vicar, unlike some of his associates, who were stiffer than the dog collar they wore around their necks. He smiled, suppressing the laughter that was threatening to bubble to the surface. "Oh dear, that is unfortunate. I'm sure there was no malice intended, knowing Arthur the way I did. He was such a cheeky chappie."

Mrs Tinder's demeanour softened as she contemplated the fondness with which he'd spoken about her deceased husband. "Thank you. He was one in a million, and I never thought I'd say this, but I miss him terribly. He was a law unto himself most of the time, but the thing I miss most is the company he gave me in the evening. Nowadays, I do everything I can not to be alone in the house, even on foul evenings like this."

He placed a hand on her forearm. "You know I'm always at the end of the phone, Mrs Tinder... sorry, Katherine. There's never a reason for you to feel alone. You're one of the most loved parishioners in our community. That much was obvious by the number of people who showed up to give Arthur the send-off he deserved."

"I know. I'll be forever grateful to the residents of this fantastic village for showing me how much he meant to everyone on the day. It wasn't the best weather for it, much like today. Anyway, you don't want to hang around here, discussing the quirks of my dearly departed husband. You should be at home with your adorable wife. She'll be wondering where you've got to. The meeting ran over an hour as it is."

"Yvonne accepts we had a full agenda to go through this evening. Had she been in better health, she would have been here, by my side. But she's been having these crippling migraines that keep her up most of the night. She went to the doctor the other day, and he gave her some strong sleeping tablets to try. As yet, she's been reluctant to take them. I think I finally persuaded her to try a couple tonight because she's been wandering around the house like a zombie. I'm not saying they'll be the answer to her problem long term, but she needs something to give her a reprieve. You know yourself how important it is to get a full night's sleep every now and again."

"I do. I suffered terribly in my early forties. In the end, I was forced to give up work because my insomnia was so debilitating that I was unable to function properly. Unfortunately, the doctors back in those days weren't as obliging as they are today. Right, I must go now."

"If you can wait five minutes, I'll walk back with you; we can share my umbrella."

Mrs Tinder smiled. "At least you had the foresight to bring one with you."

"I must admit, I should have listened to the weather forecast before setting off this evening. I probably would have thought about bringing the car instead."

3

"Such a short distance to contemplate wasting fuel these days, what with the cost of it."

"I know, but it would have kept us dry, wouldn't it? I'll just be a jiffy. I need to ensure the vestry and the back door are both locked. I know Sid went out that way earlier to put the rubbish out for me."

"He did, you're right. Is there anything else I can do for you?"

"No, you've done enough this evening as it is. Take a seat. I'll be as quick as I can."

He spun around and picked up several hymn books lying on the pews on his way through the small but perfectly formed church that was thankfully packed every Sunday. He'd been the resident vicar here for the past ten years, since moving up from London. The parishioners had made him feel welcome from day one, making the transition far easier than he and Yvonne had ever expected. Over the years, he'd heard so many horror stories about people in small communities such as Wilton, digging their heels in, not being open to welcoming outsiders, especially when the previous vicar, Mr Hartley, had been at the church for the past thirty years or so.

With his chores completed, he collected the golfing umbrella from his office, along with the bunch of keys, and returned to the main entrance.

Mrs Tinder was standing in the doorway, gauging if the rain had eased off. "It's getting worse out there, not better. Maybe we should make a run for it then. What do you think, Vicar?"

"I agree. I hope you've got your running shoes on."

"I haven't, but these will have to do. They're low enough for me not to trip over any of the dodgy pavements that the parish council keeps telling us they're going to repair and yet never seem to get around to."

He raised a hand. "Guilty as charged. I'll make sure the matter is addressed again at the next meeting we hold."

"I wish you would. I know most people use their vehicles these days, but since lockdown, I've been trying my very best to get out and about more with little Charlie trotting along beside me, but I've turned my ankle more than once on the pavement close to my bungalow. I had a word with the chairman about it; he promised me months ago that something would be done about it as a matter of urgency, but it's still in the same shocking state it has been in for the past eighteen months."

"That's terrible. It shouldn't have taken that long to fix the issue. Leave it with me. Right, are you ready to brave the elements together?"

"I'll believe it when I see it. I'm ready when you are."

He locked the door while Mrs Tinder took charge of the umbrella. He relieved her of the brolly soon after and tucked her arm through his to ensure they were both adequately covered. "We'd better put our best foot forward, Mrs Tinder. Are you up for it?"

"I agree. I'm quite fit, thanks to me getting my steps in these days with Charlie, so walk as quickly as you like. It's not like we have to go very far, is it?"

"This rain is relentless, though. It will make the journey to the end of the village a chore."

"Between us, I bet we've battled far worse than this over the years, Vicar."

He smiled and nodded. "I dare say you're right. Let's go."

They nattered about this and that, but mostly about things that had affected their respective families over the years. As expected, it didn't take them long to reach Mrs Tinder's garden gate. Paul insisted he should shield her until they reached her front door.

"Will you come in for a tea or coffee, Vicar?"

5

"It's kind of you to offer, but I believe the weather is only going to get worse, so I think I should get home now."

Mrs Tinder hopped over the front doorstep to her bungalow and waved him off. "If you insist. Say hello to that lovely wife of yours, tell her I'll pop around in the morning to see how she's getting on with the crafts I asked her to make for the church."

"Ah, yes, they're nearly finished and looking good. Praise where it's due. Enjoy the rest of your evening."

"You, too. I hope you don't end up getting too wet."

"I can dry off in front of the fire when I reach the vicarage. Take care. Thank you for your company this evening. You're a wonderful human being."

She chuckled and closed the door behind her.

Paul upped his pace, eager to get home in the dry. He could see the outdoor light was on at the vicarage up ahead of him. This part of the village wasn't well lit, and he kicked through a large puddle in the pavement outside Mrs Tinder's home, the one she'd complained about earlier. He shook the excess rain from his now-soaked feet, cursed under his breath, and continued on his walk. A car passed by slowly beside him; he was thankful the driver hadn't given him another soaking coming close to the kerb. He waved, showing his appreciation at the driver's thoughtfulness, a rarity in this day and age during weather such as this.

The vehicle stopped a few feet ahead of him. It wasn't one that he recognised, at least he didn't think so. The driver switched off the engine; maybe they were visiting Mrs Otis a few doors down. He'd visited the poor lady who was now in her nineties and bedbound only last week, to say a prayer with her and her family, not expecting her to last much longer but, according to her daughter, she had defied all the odds and was rallying, surprising them all.

Continuing his walk, he thought it strange that no one

had exited the car by the time he'd reached it. He dipped down to see if he recognised the driver and saw there were two people in the vehicle, holding a conversation. He felt foolish and continued his journey. The car started up and crept up beside him, parking ahead of him again.

Maybe they're lost and trying to pluck up the courage to ask me the way.

He reached the car once more and bent down to peer inside at the passenger. The car remained dark. Annoyance rose because the electricity company had removed every other lamppost along this stretch of the village. What use was that to the residents who walked the streets at night?

The car crept forward again, so Paul began his walk once more. This time he crossed the road, what with the vicarage being around twenty-five feet ahead of him. The car drove off, but he saw it turn around at the end of the street and come towards him, faster this time, as if it was going to drive straight past him. Nothing could be further from the truth. The car halted abruptly beside him, and the passenger door was flung open. It hit his leg with such force that he stumbled backwards into a hedge.

"Hey, why don't you watch what you're doing? You could hurt someone with your antics."

"That's the whole idea. Mouthing off again, are you, Vicar? Well, we're going to put an end to that kind of shit."

"Excuse me? Do I know you?"

The person was dressed from head to toe in black, a hood covering most of their features. Paul didn't recognise the voice; he believed the person was disguising it on purpose. He took a step towards them in the hope they would see the error of their ways and apologise for hurting him.

The opposite happened. The man lashed out with his fists. Paul was caught off-guard. He dropped the umbrella and again stumbled back against the privet hedge, which acted like ropes in a boxing ring. He bounced back, right into the path of his attacker once more. His first instinct was to protect himself from further attack, so he held his hands up in front of him.

"Please, what do you want from me?"

"Nothing. You had your chance and let us down in the worst way imaginable. Let your God save you now, if He can."

"What are you saying? If I have failed you, please give me the chance to put things right. No one is perfect in this life, even vicars."

"You're not wrong there." The assailant took another swipe at him. This time he had a knife in his hand, and the blade sliced through Paul's cassock and the sweatshirt beneath. Blood saturated his clothing within seconds. He placed a hand over his midriff and gasped.

"What have you done? Why?"

"Because we can. We're not here to debate things with you. You've had your chance in the past few months to put things right, but you've neglected your duties, and now you're going to pay for failing your parishioners, the very people who held you in high regard because of your position within this village. There are some of us who have had enough of your charade, the lies that fall out of your mouth. And you, a man of God! People believe every word you say, but you're no better than the others. If anything, you're the worst one, and that's why you need to be punished. You spout poison every damn week, and there are gullible individuals, like sweet Mrs Tinder, who believe everything that comes out of that mouth of yours. You should be ashamed of the lies you tell while wearing your dog collar. Ashamed, I said, but you will never show any remorse for the way you treat people."

Paul held his arms out to the sides and shrugged. "Please,

I don't have a clue what you're talking about. Come back to the vicarage with me, we'll discuss the issues you have over a pot of tea."

"Ha, how naïve of you to consider that a possibility at this late stage in the proceedings. No, the time for talking was over long ago, for us anyway. Clearly, you only want to open your door to us when the chips are down, and you feel there is no other option for you."

"That's totally untrue. Talk to me, we can overcome all of this and move on with a structured plan in place."

The assailant tipped his head back, ensuring his hood didn't move to reveal his features. "I've told you already, the time for talking has distanced itself. This is our moment to take revenge, and you're going to be the first on the list."

"What are you talking about? Revenge for what?" Paul glanced up and down the road, hoping someone would see what was going on and come to his rescue. However, the weather had put paid to any form of rescue coming his way, and he knew that.

"You've had your chance to put things right for us, for the community, but you failed us, and now we're going to take revenge for all those in the parish who you have let down, gravely let down."

"How? Allow me to make amends, please." The loss of blood was affecting his ability to remain upright; it was also telling in his voice.

"Gone, gone, gone, the time for talking has long since passed. It's our time to flourish. To take back what you have stripped from us over the past few months, the chance to speak up for ourselves. To take action where folks like you have failed us. You're corrupt personified, and useless in your undertaking to speak out against those who have sinned against us. We despise you with every breath we take. You were there to protect us, and you let us down, not once, twice, or even three times. You've damaged this community and the residents in more ways than you can imagine. The stress you've put us under…"

"I don't know what you mean. Please, I'm losing a lot of blood, it's affecting my ability to stand, you have to get me to the hospital. Do that, and I promise to help you."

"Tick tock, time is running out for you, Vicar, in more ways than one. You've failed your flock, and you're going to suffer the consequences."

"But how?" he pleaded, aware that his life depended on his ability to turn this situation on its head quickly.

"You make me sick, pleading ignorance to what has taken place, even when your life depends on it. Your morals suck, and they will continue to suck until you take your final breath."

Heart racing and his breathing coming in short bursts, Paul held out a hand to plead for his life. "Please, I've got no idea what you're talking about. Why don't you come out and say it? Either that or get me to the hospital before I pass out. I'm losing more blood every second I stand here arguing the toss with you. I don't know you, therefore, I can't help with your problem. I'm fading fast, won't you help me?"

The man took a step forward and slapped Paul on the back. "Of course I can help you. Except I won't be calling you an ambulance, I have other plans for you."

"What have I ever done to you? Why are you so intent on hurting me? Killing me? That is what you're saying?"

"Finally, the penny drops. That's why I have no intention of calling an ambulance because we have much more appropriate plans in mind for you." He opened the passenger door again and bent down to speak to the driver. "Meet us over at the vicarage. The vicar and I will join you over there." He slammed the door shut again, gripped Paul by the elbow and steered him towards the vicarage over twenty-five feet away.

"I'm sorry, I can't do this... walk any further."

"Come now, Vicar, don't try to pull the wool over my eyes, I've seen you power walking your way around the village every other day and cycling for miles on end as well. You're fit, and here you are, trying to tell me you're incapable of walking the rest of the way to your home. What kind of fool are you taking me for?"

"Yes, I'm fit, but I also have a large gash in my stomach and have probably lost a couple of pints of blood in the last five minutes."

"Excuses, excuses. You're full of them, aren't you? You and your tight buddies on the parish council. That's all this village has heard from your mob the last few months, a bunch of excuses as to why... Never mind, I shouldn't have to spell out what all this is about. The time for talking is over and done with. Now it's time for you to pay the price... all of you."

"Wait? If you have an issue that you wish to discuss, to find a solution to even, then please, let's sit down like civilised human beings and have that discussion."

"It's too late. The time for debating the issue has passed. It's been finalised by you and your mob without any consideration for the villagers who you are supposed to represent."

"If this is... ouch..." The leg which the attacker had struck with the car door suddenly gave way beneath him, and he ended up in another hedge, which this time was full of thorns.

His assailant yanked him to his feet again. "I sense you're intent on playing games with me, pretending to be hurt. Why? Are you hoping God will intervene?"

"No, I'm hurt. I defy any man with a gash in his stomach to be able to walk in a straight line for long. Please, help me. Take me to the hospital, and nothing more will be said about this."

"Shut up and move."

The man shoved Paul in the back. He dragged his injured leg and hobbled towards what he classed as his family home, scared of what would happen to his wife and son when he got there. He had to delay the inevitable as much as he could.

But he sensed the man provoking him had other plans, such as a second shove and another dig with the blade jabbed in his back. He would cry out, but what was the point during this foul weather? No one was going to hear or see him or even come to his rescue.

Sadly, before long, they had reached the grounds of the vicarage. Yvonne had left the light on in the porch, but it was the only sign of life in the property.

Why did I force her to take a tablet tonight? Why did she have to be asleep? If she is asleep, I hope she is, for her sake. I wouldn't want her to witness my death. What if the people doing this turn their attention on Yvonne after they've killed me? I can't allow that to happen. I just can't. I need to stand up and be a man. If that means forgetting that I'm a man of the cloth, then so be it. I need to fight for my life. It's the only way I'm going to get out of this mess, isn't it?

They ventured further into the immaculate garden, which his wife took great care attending to during every spare minute she had in her day. Behind him, the car door slammed. Soon after, the driver joined them. The attackers put their heads together, probably going over their plan, whatever that might be. Paul glanced around; he inched towards a metal pole he knew he'd hidden under the nearby hedge, only for a voice to interrupt his thoughts.

"We know what you're up to. If you don't accept your fate with dignity, I'm warning you, we'll march into the house, get your family out of their beds and kill them alongside you. No, on second thoughts, they'll die before you, and you'll be forced to watch them suffer. Tell me, Vicar, is that what you truly want?"

"No. What I really want is for you to think about what you're doing here tonight. The reality of this unspeakable situation. How many people are going to suffer just because I've upset you? If only you would tell me what this was all about, I would do my very best to put things right, but you're not allowing me to do that, are you?"

"I don't enjoy repeating myself, but you're forcing me to. The time for talking is over. Hey, you should be happy about this next step. You're about to meet your maker, and no amount of praying on your part is going to change the inevitable. Isn't that what every vicar wants at the end of the day? To be sitting alongside his God? They're rhetorical questions; don't bother answering. I sense that only more lies will pour out of your mouth." The man turned to his partner and said, "Get the ropes out of the car."

The driver, who was considerably shorter, ran to the boot and removed a black bag from it. The driver struggled to carry it and ended up dragging it back to where the passenger was holding Paul. "Watch him while I get things organised."

The driver shuffled closer to Paul. They had taken the knife from the passenger and were holding the blade close to Paul's ribs, rendering him helpless. His fear leapt to another level when a thick rope with a noose at one end was removed from the black sack, along with some smaller ropes.

"Right, let's move him over to the right, get him beneath the tree."

Paul felt the need to speak out, to beg for his life. "No, don't do this. We can talk about your issues. I'll help you any way I can to get them sorted, but please let me live. I have work left to do. My time isn't up yet."

"Says you. We think… no, we know differently. Now shut up and accept your fate like a man."

Paul shook his head, trying to rid himself of the abhorrent thoughts running through his mind. As the noose was placed around his neck, he pleaded for his life once more, only to be ignored.

He was positioned beneath the tree. The attacker threw the rope at a thick branch above him; it clattered to the ground beside Paul. The relief was instant; nevertheless, it turned out to be short-lived, because when the man attempted a second time, the rope remained hooked on the branch. Despite not wanting to look up, the temptation proved to be too much. Paul didn't shout or scream—what would be the point? No one would hear him, not in this weather. He accepted his fate, closed his eyes and prayed to God that his end would come quickly.

CHAPTER 1

*D*etective Inspector Sara Ramsey was wrapping up the morning team meeting when the phone rang on Detective Sergeant Jill Smalling's desk.

Sara stopped talking and listened in to the conversation Jill was having; she couldn't help it. Something in her gut was telling her that Jill was about to inform them of a new case.

The room fell silent. Sara sensed the rest of the team was feeling the same.

Jill concentrated on the call, her head bowed, taking notes. Eventually, she hung up and said, "Sorry, ma'am. The pathologist said she didn't want to speak to you personally because of what was going on at the scene."

Sara took a few steps towards Jill. "Another case?"

"Yes, out at Wilton?"

Sara frowned and glanced at her partner, Carla Jameson, for clarification.

"I know it. It's about twenty minutes north of here," Carla confirmed.

"Okay, let's get over there, Carla, see what's different about this case that Lorraine struggled to tell me herself."

Jill passed Sara the sheet of paper with the address on. Sara took one look at it and, in a hushed voice, read it out, "The Vicarage at Wilton."

"Holy shit!" Carla peered over her shoulder and whispered.

"My thoughts exactly. Are you ready to rumble?"

"I need to nip to the ladies' first."

"Make it snappy. Jill, will you and Christine carry out the normal checks for me? I'm going to need that information ASAP."

Christine moved her chair closer to Jill. They both gave her the thumbs-up and put their heads together.

"Let's pre-empt things a little here, Craig. I need you to do the necessary regarding any CCTV in the area."

Craig chewed on his lip. "Umm… without checking, I'm inclined to think there won't be any knowing where Wilton is situated. It's a small community. I doubt if any CCTV will be set up out there."

Sara kicked out at a chair. "And there was me trying to get ahead of the game. Okay, hold fire on that for now. Get Wilton up on the map. I need you to study it while we're out. We're going into this investigation blind."

"I know. Leave it with me, boss. I'm sure I'll come up with something we can use," Craig assured her.

Carla returned and collected her jacket from the back of the chair.

Sara unhooked her woollen coat from the stand close to her office and slipped it on. "Right, we're off. As soon as we know what we're dealing with, we'll get back to you."

"Good luck," Barry shouted as they passed.

"Thanks. I need the rest of you to go over any outstanding paperwork. You know how much I hate loose ends hanging around when we take on another case."

"Leave it with us, boss," Marissa said.

. . .

As PREDICTED, they arrived at the vicarage nearly twenty minutes later, thanks to Carla's impeccable navigational skills.

"How do you know this place?" Sara asked. "I don't remember us ever coming out this way, not since I moved here."

"Mum used to have a friend who lived out here. She had a daughter my age; we used to play in the garden while Mum and her friend caught up on life."

"That sounds so sweet," Sara said. Nothing had ever happened like that in her childhood, not that she could remember.

"It wasn't. The girl detested me, and, in turn, because of the vile things she did to me when we were out of sight of our mothers, I hated her, too."

"Never! What type of things?"

"She threw me into the large pond they had, which was full of toads. I freaked out and couldn't stop screaming."

"Oh damn, I think I would have pushed her in, exacting my revenge."

"Don't think the thought hadn't crossed my mind."

"What else did the little bitch do?"

"It had been raining the day before we visited; they had a small paddock where they kept two ponies. She invited me to go down there to see them. Which I did. The cow tripped me up as soon as we entered the field. I ended up face down in a pile of manure."

"What the fuck? And what was your reaction?"

"I was mortified, desperate to wipe the floor with her, but Mum would have annihilated me if I had retaliated. The bitch pleaded with me, told me it was a genuine mistake, and even offered to shake my hand. I did that all right after I'd removed the shit from my clothes. Her face was a picture. I smiled, daring her to tell on me. We seemed to get on better after that day, you know, after defining our limits and boundaries."

Sara laughed. "I can imagine. Have you had the pleasure of seeing her since?"

"I haven't. Last I heard, she was doing a ten-year stretch for manslaughter."

Sara twisted in her seat, her mouth gaping open. She shook her head and said, "What? You're kidding me?"

Carla smiled. "Yep. You can be so gullible at times."

Her partner's comment earned her a slap on the thigh. "Bugger, I believed you there—only for a second, though."

They exited the car and met up at the boot, where they pulled on a protective suit. "Yeah, right. You fell for it, hook, line and sinker. Go on, admit it. Actually, you don't have to, it was written all over your face."

The gravel crunched behind them. "Morning, ladies. I hate to break up what appears to be a joyful scene."

"Sorry, Lorraine. It's her fault, winding me up, as usual." Sara jabbed a thumb in Carla's direction.

Sighing, the pathologist said, "I'm going to need you to slip into professional mode ASAP, ladies."

"We're there, I promise. What have you got for us?"

"We received a call first thing. I'm surprised they didn't notify you about the case sooner. It might be something you should look into when you get back."

"We'll do that. What have we got?" Sara glanced over Lorraine's shoulder at the tent that had been erected.

"The wife was very distraught when we got here, for obvious reasons. Her husband is the local vicar—correction, he used to be. When we showed up, he was swinging in the breeze, a well-constructed noose tied around his neck."

"Oh heck. How long had he been there, do you know?"

18

"I'm guessing overnight, but hopefully, the PM will tell me more. Do you want to see him?"

"If that's okay with you? Are you all right, Lorraine?"

"Not really. I detest it when a man of the cloth is murdered. I can see no rhyme or reason for a vicar's life to be ended unless he was a dubious character, of course."

Sara rubbed the pathologist's upper arm. "I'm sorry this has affected you like this."

"I'll get over it... you know, live to fight another day. The same can't be said for the victim." Lorraine led the way over to the marquee and flicked back the flap for them to enter. "Come in. We're lucky the tree sheltered the ground, otherwise, we'd be kneeling in mud by now."

Sara studied the victim, who had been cut down and was lying on the ground. In his late forties, he had greying hair and a small goatee beard that emphasised his handsome features.

"I take it the cause of death was hanging?"

"Yes, although he had a gaping wound in his stomach. I'm presuming the injury occurred up the road, judging by the trail of blood we found."

"Even in the vile weather last night?"

"Yes, there are ways and means. The rain ceased at about eleven, according to my app."

"So, he was killed sometime before that? Attacked by someone and then brought here and hanged from the tree, in familiar surroundings?"

"Yep, hard to believe, right?"

"Somewhat. Didn't the wife hear anything?"

"No, she's got insomnia. Last night, her husband made her take a couple of tablets to help her sleep. She took them at around nine-thirty, and they knocked her out instantly. She woke up at eight this morning, drew back the curtains and got the shock of her life."

Sara's gaze drifted back to the victim. "Oh shit, that poor woman. Was she alone in the house?"

"No, her son was with her. They're both inside, waiting to speak with you."

"Bugger, okay. What else can you tell us, Lorraine, anything?"

"Not really, except this was obviously a premeditated murder, judging by the rope the killer or killers used."

"The fact they brought it along with them," Sara mumbled, more to herself.

"How awful," Carla replied. "Who could have enough hate in them to go after a vicar?"

"That's what we're going to need to find out," Sara replied. She glanced down at the victim as if searching for clues from him. "I'm with you, Lorraine. I also hate it when a clergyman is targeted. I suppose they're more susceptible than others because of their role in the community."

"Sadly true, although I wish it wasn't." Lorraine bent down beside the corpse. "I believe the wound to his stomach was supposed to debilitate him. He seems pretty fit to me. He didn't have an ounce of fat on him. Maybe that's what the killer was worried about, him retaliating and having the strength to overpower him, hence the killer's need to slice his stomach open."

"Either way, what you're telling us is that he suffered immensely before he finally took his last breath."

"Yes, that's what I think. Bugger, I hate cases like this, where the wife is the one who discovers her husband's body. Such an unnecessary evil."

"I agree. Any other injuries that you can see?"

"Not yet."

"Okay, we're going to brave it, go inside and speak to the wife. How old is the son?" Sara asked. She walked back towards the flap and swept it aside.

"Hmm... mid-twenties."

"What's your instinct about him? Could this be to do with him?"

Lorraine stood and held her arms out to the sides. "That's your department, not mine. Good luck; he's a feisty sort, so tread carefully."

"Message received and understood, thanks. We'll drop back and see you after we've spoken to the family."

"If we're still on site. I want to get him out of here as soon as we can. I've looked up at the house a few times and caught the wife standing at the window, watching us."

"Creepy, but I suppose it's a natural instinct to want to see what's going on."

Carla followed Sara out of the marquee, and they stripped off their protective clothing, deposited it in a black bag, and then made their way over to the house. Sara rang the bell.

"It'll be the police. Are you coming down, Mum?" Sara heard the son say from the hallway.

"Yes."

A young blond man in his mid-twenties opened the door and checked their IDs before he allowed them to enter the large hallway. A woman in a silk robe descended the stairs, nodded at them and walked into the nearest room on the left.

"That's Mum. She's all over the place at the moment. I've tried encouraging her to get dressed, but she keeps telling me to leave her alone. Can I get you both a drink? I was about to make us one before you arrived, so it's no bother."

"Thanks. Milk and one sugar in both. Shall we go through and introduce ourselves to your mother?" Sara asked, already inching her way towards the room.

"Yes, go through. It might be a bit dark in there. I've pulled the curtains so we don't have to see what's going on outside."

"We understand, don't worry."

"I'm not. I'll be with you in a second. Make yourselves comfortable."

Sara knocked on the door before she entered the room, but the woman didn't answer. Popping her head around the door, Sara asked, "Is it all right if we come in?"

The woman was standing by the bay window, peering around the curtain. "Yes, do what you like."

"I'm DI Sara Ramsey, and this is my partner, DS Carla Jameson. My advice would be to leave them to it. They'll be packing up soon, taking your husband to the mortuary."

"What? They can't. Don't I have to give them permission to take him away?"

The three of them sat, and Sara answered, "No, it's a crime scene. I'm afraid you don't have any say in what takes place now."

"Is that how it's going to be? My son and I are going to be pushed aside as if we don't matter?"

"No, not at all. I'm sorry, I didn't catch your name."

"It's Yvonne Gains. The victim was my darling husband, Paul Gains. I know you're going to ask me if I know who did this, but the truth is, no, I haven't got a clue. My husband was a good man, obviously. He loved being a member of this community. Nothing like this, you know what I mean, has ever happened before. Everyone has always treated him kindly. I don't know who could have done this, not to my darling Paul." She broke down and covered her face with her hands.

Carla withdrew her notebook from her pocket and flipped it open. Sara handed the woman a box of tissues from the coffee table.

Sara paused before she asked, "He hasn't fallen out with the neighbours or anyone in the village?"

"No, Paul wasn't the type. I know some vicars can be a tad

offish with their parishioners. Paul was different, he always went out of his way to help people, as any good Christian person would."

"When was the last time you spoke to him, in person?"

"Around six last night, he had a meeting at the church."

Sara shuffled forward to the edge of the fabric sofa. "A meeting? Regarding?"

"It's coming up to the busiest time of the year, Christmas. There are lots of things to organise, what songs to sing for midnight mass, that type of thing."

"How many people were due to attend the meeting?"

"I don't know, maybe twenty-five to thirty. But I don't believe any of them would sink to this level and kill Paul. It has to be an outsider."

The door opened, and in walked the son, carrying a tray with four mugs on it, which he placed on the coffee table between all the seats. "What have I interrupted?" He handed everyone a mug.

Yvonne put her mug on the coffee table beside her. "The officers asked how many people attended the church meeting last night."

"Ah, right. It's usually a good turnout. I haven't been to one in a while, but Dad said he was expecting around thirty people."

"Any reason why you didn't go?" Sara held her mug and ignored the chocolate biscuits sitting on the tray.

"No, I was at the college. I'm taking a woodworking course there. Dad was quite handy and was encouraging me to be the same."

"I detect an accent. Are you from around here?"

"No, we're originally from Kent. We've been here for about ten years, never dreamt anything like this would be the way my father departed this world."

Yvonne reached for her son's hand.

Sara offered a slight smile. "Sorry, you are?"

"I'm Danny, Daniel, but I hate it. Much prefer to be called Danny."

"He was named after Paul's grandfather."

"I see. And you live here, along with your parents?" Sara asked.

"Yes. Mum and Dad are, were, very easy-going. They let me do what I want, when I want, within reason, so I haven't felt the need to move out. I couldn't afford it, not with the cost of living the way it is."

"We're happy to look after our son until he's ready to move out. His girlfriend, Cassie, is a sweetheart. They're eager to set up home together, but neither of them is earning enough money to cover the basic bills needed to survive these days. Or we were before Paul's... death. When will you be able to tell us who did this, and more to the point, why?"

"I think it would be better if you asked how long a piece of string is. I don't mean to be flippant, but with little to no clues to go on, it's impossible to give you a definitive answer."

"So, what's your first step in an investigation of this nature?" Danny asked. His gaze held Sara's as he took a sip of his coffee.

"Well, it depends on what evidence presented itself at the scene, if any. If SOCO didn't find anything and nothing shows up during the post-mortem, we'll need to contact everyone who knew your father, starting with members of the community who attended the meeting held at the church last night."

"But that could mean you interviewing thousands of people," Danny replied, his brow creased.

Sara shrugged. "Some investigations take months to pull together, and others are often solved within a few weeks, if we're lucky. As I said, it depends on what evidence or clues are available to us. Initially, we'll flood the area with uniformed officers, going house to house, to check if the neighbours or any of the residents in the village saw anything out of the ordinary last night. A stranger walking past, an unusual vehicle in the area, anything along those lines. Were you both here last night?"

"Yes. Mum took a sleeping pill. You went to bed at about nine-thirty, didn't you, Mum?"

"That's right."

"And what about you, Danny?" Sara asked. She wondered where his feistiness had disappeared to that Lorraine had warned her about because he'd cooperated with her until now.

"I was listening to music in my room until the early hours of the morning. Just to clarify, I had my headphones on so I didn't disturb Mum."

"Understood, and did you leave your room at all? Possibly to check whether your father had got home safely?"

"Are you kidding me? Last time I had a conversation with him, he was forty-eight years old, not a teenager."

And there it is… maybe I should give him the benefit of the doubt in the circumstances.

"Danny, don't start. The officer is only trying to do her job. She can't do that without asking the proper questions. We need to keep a cool head."

Danny slowly turned to face his mother; his eyes narrowed as if he were furious with her for making a show of him in front of company. "A cool head? Let's see this for what it is, Mum. It's a damn murder investigation. Someone out there killed my father." His gaze drifted back to Sara, his eyes remaining tiny slits. "And I'm telling you this, if you don't pull your fingers out and capture the fucker who did this by the end of the week…"

Sara inclined her head and said, "Don't stop there, Danny. What will you do?"

"Your frigging job for you. Except I won't be handing the culprit over to you lot for you to put through this joke of a justice system we've got nowadays. Nope, I'll tear the fucker from limb to limb and scatter the pieces in different parts of the country."

His mother started sobbing. "Danny, why are you so angry? Your father has been taken from us barely twelve hours ago, and here you are, swearing like a trooper on a hot day in the midday sun. He'd be mortified to hear such language coming out of that mouth of yours. We've strived to give you everything we could over the years, sent you to the best schools we could afford on our paltry income, and to hear you speak now... I have no further words to describe your intolerable behaviour. I think you should leave the room immediately. Let me talk to the officers alone if that's the sort of language that is going to spill out of your mouth."

Yvonne glared at her son, and he stared back just as hard.

Finally, he shrugged, sat back in the easy chair, and crossed his arms in defiance. "I'm staying, whether you like it or not. He was my father, and I demand to know what these officers intend doing about finding his killer."

"I'm sorry," Yvonne apologised.

"I should think so. I didn't deserve to be on the receiving end of an outburst like that, Mother."

Yvonne sucked in a large breath. "I wasn't apologising to you. I was saying sorry to the inspector and her partner. They don't need to hear the crap you spouted. You've been all talk and no action since you were in your teens. It was often a conversation your father and I had between us."

Danny bounced forward again, an evil glint in his eye. "You what? How can you say that? Ah, I see. It's all coming out now that the peacemaker is no longer with us, isn't it? You've always hated me. Come on, you might as well come right out and say it."

"Don't be so ridiculous. You're twisting my words to make me look bad. Why don't you leave me to deal with the police? Go on, get out."

He grinned and shook his head slowly in response. "I'm not going anywhere. I have every right to know what happened to my father."

Sara raised her hands. "I'm sorry, that's just not true, Danny. Your mother is your father's next of kin, she has the right to tell you to leave the room or not. It's her we've come to see."

His head jutted forward. "You're unbelievable. I knew you women would stick together. No surprise there."

"Grow up, Danny. Now, please, leave us alone. I'm struggling to deal with my emotions as it is now, because of your childish, selfish behaviour... nope, I'm not going there. I'm requesting that you leave me to speak with the police. If I need your help, I'll give you a shout."

His gaze locked on to each of them, but eventually, he marched out of the room and slammed the door behind him.

Yvonne flinched and began sobbing once more. "I'm so sorry. You shouldn't have witnessed that. Our, my son's character can be unpredictable at times. I can only see things getting worse between us. His father was the one who used to keep him in line. Paul had a greater understanding of his needs, shall we say?"

"Is your son ill?"

"He's bipolar and also has ADHD, a combination that has always tested our limits. I know I shouldn't really say that. He's our, my son, and I love him dearly, but he often intentionally sets out to test us." She glanced at the door, leaned forward, and lowered her voice. "He used to set us off against each other. Tell tales that were untrue. Things I'd said to him were often turned upside down. Paul and I learnt early on that it was best to agree with him to his face and to discuss the situation fully when he wasn't around."

"I see. Do you believe he's got it in him to cause us problems?"

Yvonne sighed. "Had you asked me that yesterday, I would have told you no, but who knows how his father's death is going to affect him now? What I know is that I haven't got the patience to deal with him at the moment, as heartless as that may sound. We've had a trying time with him, and now I'm going to have my husband's funeral to deal with, no mean feat, as I'm sure you'll agree."

"I'm sorry you have to contend with all of this on your own. Do you have any other family living close by?"

"My sister, Janice, she lives in Worcester. I'll call her once you leave and see if she has the time to come and be with me. She runs her own business, a boutique in the city centre, so I don't like to burden her with our troubles, not really, because she has enough on her plate as it is."

"Does she have a member of staff who could take over for a few days?"

"I'm not sure. I'll have to call her. I'll do that later. I need to know if there's anything else I can help you with."

Sara's heart went out to the woman. "We can arrange for a family liaison officer to be involved; they can ease the pressure on your shoulders."

"Thank you, but I'm going to have to decline your offer because Danny has been known to become violent when there are strangers in the house."

"We wouldn't want to cause any extra inconvenience to either of you. The offer is on the table, should you change your mind. I have to ask, you mentioned that you and your husband had a trying time with your son. Can you tell us more?"

"The doctor changed his medication, and it had a devastating effect on him. His temperament went from one end of the spectrum to the other. He became violent a few times and broke a couple of windows in the house. I couldn't cope with him when my husband wasn't around. In the end, Paul demanded to see the doctor and asked him if Danny's medication had been altered. The doctor admitted that he was trialling a new drug on the market. They never consider the family. We're the ones who had to suffer with the consequences, not him. Thoughtless and irresponsible, and I took great pleasure in telling him that when I marched down there to the surgery. A week of taking those drugs set Danny back several years, and no, that's not an exaggeration, it's a fact."

"That's terrible. I'm so sorry you, as a family, had to go through such a traumatic experience. Did Danny do anything outside the home? Umm… I didn't really word that right, I apologise. Let me try again. After Danny broke the windows in your home, did he leave the house and cause any problems outside, possibly in the community?"

Yvonne rubbed at her temple and considered the question. "I don't think so. We tried to keep him contained in the house. By that, I'm not saying we locked him in. We didn't go that far because it would have had an adverse effect on him."

"Does Danny work?"

"He volunteers a day or so each week at an animal sanctuary."

"And how does he get on there?"

"Very well. It would appear that he has an affinity with animals. We've adopted two kittens from there over the last few months. Thankfully, they love being outdoors for most of the day, then he brings them in at teatime and takes them up to his room at night when he retires to bed."

"Do they calm him down?"

"Yes, they seem to."

Sara smiled. "You also mentioned he has a girlfriend. How long have they been seeing each other?"

"About a year. She's more like a friend than a girlfriend. She suffers from ADHD as well."

"Ah, I see. Bear with me here; do you think anything your son might have done could be responsible for what happened to your husband?"

"No, definitely not." Yvonne fell silent and then whispered, "I bloody well hope not, but who knows? How can we tell? I can't come out and ask him. He's too volatile and would lash out if I questioned him too much. He often feels backed into a corner. Therefore, it's crucial to know his emotional state before asking questions."

"Are you saying that we wouldn't stand a chance interviewing Danny, then?"

"Yes, there's no way you'd be able to do it."

"Not even with you present?"

"Possibly, but then you saw what his reaction was like before."

"We'll leave things as they are for now, then, although we're going to need a list of names of those who attended the meeting last night, if you have it?"

"It'll be in my husband's office. Let me see if I can find it for you."

"If you wouldn't mind, thank you."

Yvonne wiped her eyes on a tissue, sipped at her drink, then left the room. She closed the door behind her, allowing Sara and Carla to have a quick conversation in her absence.

"Wow, what did you make of the son?"

Carla chewed her lip. "I think we need to tread carefully there. I know Lorraine warned us he was a feisty character, but we witnessed a different side to him—well, up until he lost it with his mother, I just thought he was normal."

"I know. I struggled to believe what Lorraine had said until he erupted like Mount Vesuvius."

"Christ, if I'd ever spoken to my mother like that, let's just say I would need a doctor to give me the all-clear."

Sara laughed. "That bad, eh? I'm wondering if he's done something to upset someone, and that person came back and took it out on his father."

"It's a possibility, but how the hell are we going to find out?"

Sara glanced around the room and puffed out her cheeks. "Ask me something I can give you an answer to." She spotted a family photo on the windowsill and crossed the room to inspect it. Sara could tell that the vicar was a gentle person. There was kindness in his eyes. The family appeared to look happy in the photo, which she thought was a recent one. "Hard to believe that he's now dead. He seems so full of life, and they all look really happy."

"I hope this doesn't turn out to be a long, drawn-out investigation, or worse still, one that we never get around to solving. I don't think that's going to do Yvonne and Danny's relationship any good in the long run."

Sara replaced the photo on the windowsill and returned to her seat. "I agree. I keep coming back to the fact that the crime was premeditated, and it's a hard one to shift."

"Yeah. I suppose we'll know more once we start speaking to the neighbours and the residents in the village who knew him well."

Sara didn't get the chance to say anything further because Yvonne entered. She returned to her seat and passed the manilla folder to Sara.

"It's all in there; actually, I've added another list of all those who tend to show up at the church every Sunday."

"That's extremely helpful, thank you. I was admiring the photo over there. May I ask when it was taken?"

"Ah yes, that's one of my favourites. My sister took it when we visited Worcester about six months ago. It was a lovely day out. Even Danny enjoyed himself. The day trip happened before his change of medication. So, you can see the difference in him. He was always smiling. Not that I'm saying he's a miserable bugger now. He's not, most of the time." She sighed heavily. "Why doctors have to fiddle with people's medication is beyond me. Why don't they just leave well alone? Bloody idiots. Like I said earlier, they're not the ones who have to deal with the consequences. That's down to the family."

"It is remarkable, the change in him. We've witnessed that firsthand. Has Danny had any problems with anyone living in the village over the years?"

"He was bullied as a child, but name me someone who hasn't been."

"Because of his ADHD?"

"Yes, he was a slow learner. The kids used to call him thick—he's not, far from it. He's a very intelligent young man, but sometimes he struggles with how to express himself. That's when the frustration kicks in and the anger surfaces."

"I can understand that. Does he have many friends in the village?"

"No, not really. He'll say hello to people he knows, although he has a girlfriend. As for making solid friendships, no, I don't think that's ever been on the cards."

"That's a shame. So, you're a close family, most of the time?"

"Yes, exceptionally. I know it doesn't seem like it, with the way I spoke to him, but these are exceptional circumstances, and I'm not sure how I'm supposed to react after losing my husband in such a horrendous way. Nothing can prepare you for this, I assure you."

Sara smiled and patted the woman's hand. "I know, and I appreciate it. Try not to overthink things. I'm sure Danny will come round soon."

"He came to see me when I was in the office. We had a cuddle. I told him everything was going to be all right, but I'm not sure if I did the right thing or not, saying that, because it's never going to be all right again."

"No, that's true. You're both going to need to learn how to adapt; it will not be easy, far from it. Don't forget my offer is still on the table for a family liaison officer to be here with you."

"Thank you, I'll consider it, amongst everything else in my life that is about to change. Maybe I should call my sister sooner rather than later. I don't think I'm going to cope otherwise."

"Would you like me to ring your sister?"

"Maybe that would be wise. I don't think I'd be able to hold it together long enough to tell her what's happened."

"Don't worry, leave it with me. Can I have her number?"

Yvonne reached down beside her chair and removed her phone from her handbag. After scrolling through it, she dialled a number. "Here, you can use mine."

She quickly passed the phone to Sara, who rushed out of the room to take the call in the hallway.

"Hi, Sis, what's up? Long time no hear."

"Hi, Janice. You don't know me. I'm Detective Inspector Sara Ramsey."

"What? What's going on? Where's Yvonne? Has she been hurt? My God, I'm coming right over there. I'll shut up shop and can be there within half an hour if I put my foot down."

"Umm... I wouldn't advise speeding. Please, Yvonne is okay, but there is something important that I need to tell you."

"Thank God for that. But if she's okay, I don't understand why a police officer would be calling me on her phone. Care to enlighten me?"

"Absolutely. I have some bad news for you."

"Is it Danny? Has something happened to him? I know he's not the best communicator in the world and can often come across as angry, but his heart is in the right place."

"No, he's fine. However..."

"That only leaves Paul. Please tell me!"

Sara closed her eyes and told the woman the truth. "It's with regret that I have to tell you Paul was murdered last night."

"Last night! He what? Do you mind repeating that? Because for a second or two there, I thought you said that he'd been murdered. Tell me I misheard you."

"You didn't. I'm sorry to be the one to break the news to you, but Yvonne didn't think she had it in her to tell you. I hope you understand?"

"Oh my, I think I need to sit down. My legs have gone all wobbly."

Sara heard a chair being scraped across what sounded like a wooden floor. "Take your time. I know this can't be easy. Are you all right?"

"The honest answer is, I don't know. Am I? Have you caught the bastard who did this?"

"Not yet. Our investigation only started about an hour ago."

"Do you know who did it? Did anyone see them kill Paul? Wait, you said it happened last night... why am I only just hearing about this now?"

"That's correct, although his body was found this morning."

"By whom?"

"Unfortunately, it was Yvonne who discovered her husband's body."

"Holy shit. I'm not surprised she's devastated. I have to ask; how did he die?"

"He was found hanging from the tree in the garden."

"Bloody hell. Who would do such a thing? Why?"

"We're at a loss to know who or why at present. The facts as we know them are that Paul attended a meeting at the church last night. The weather here was atrocious, not sure what it was like over your way."

"The same. What does that matter?"

"All I'm saying is that it's likely going to prove difficult to find anyone who might have seen Paul last night as he travelled home."

"On foot or by car?"

"I haven't got around to asking Yvonne the ins and outs yet. The reason I'm calling you is to see if you wouldn't mind coming over to be with her."

"Of course, that goes without saying. I'll have to arrange cover for the shop. Can you give me an hour or so?"

"Yes, take your time."

"Where's Danny? Isn't he there with his mum?"

Sara sighed. "He is, but they've had a bit of a falling-out. Things were said, and his mother asked him to leave the room."

"Sounds about right. Paul was always the one who kept their relationship on the straight and narrow. Danny is the type of boy—sorry, I sometimes forget how old he is, young man—who shoots from the hip and asks questions later."

"Yes, that's the impression we got earlier. Thank you for agreeing to come over. I'll tell Yvonne to expect you soon. I

won't put any time frame on it, just in case. Please drive carefully. Watch out for the roadworks as you approach Hereford. They've been up there for weeks and are a pain in the
rear at certain times of the day."

"Thank you. I will take things easy. Give my love to
Yvonne, tell her I'm sorry for her loss."

"I will. See you soon."

"Thank you for calling."

Sara ended the call and, as she was at the bottom of the
stairs, she took a moment to listen for any movement going
on above. Hearing nothing, she returned to the lounge. "Your
sister sends her love."

"Is she coming over?" Yvonne asked, a tissue winding
through her finger.

"Yes, she's going to try to get someone to cover the shop
for her, and then she's going to get on the road."

"I bet she was shocked to hear the news, wasn't she?"

"She was. She asked after you and Danny."

"That was kind of her. She has a love-hate relationship
with Danny."

"Oh, may I ask why?" Sara asked, her interest piqued.

"Mainly because she doesn't understand him, or rather,
the condition he has to live with."

"Ah, yes, I can understand how that might be an issue
now and again."

"Unless people have to live with the disorder daily, it's
difficult to make them see how debilitating it can be. I don't
know how I'm going to cope now that Paul has gone. They
were so close. I'd say more like brothers than father and son,
and yes, sometimes I felt like an outsider. I know I shouldn't
say that, but it's the truth."

"Have you found that to be awkward over the years?"

"I did, in the beginning, but as the years passed, I got used
to it. I desperately wanted another child, but I couldn't stand

the thought of them being different, if you will. It was obvious from the time he was around two there was something wrong with him, but neither Paul nor I could put our finger on what was actually wrong, and the doctor was worse than hopeless at the time."

"That's a shame. I'm sorry, I've never had to deal with anyone living with the disorder, not personally. Is there any way Danny could have harmed his father without him realising it?"

She adamantly shook her head. "Definitely not, and the way Paul was murdered... no, I doubt if Danny would have had the strength to do that to his father."

"Did Paul walk to the church last night or take the car?"

"He walked there; we're quite green in that respect. Always walk where we can if our destination is within thirty minutes from the house, especially Paul. He liked to keep fit. If he didn't walk, sometimes he would take his bike instead."

"Even if it's bad weather, like last night?"

"I warned him it was going to get worse later, but he told me it didn't matter and took an umbrella with him, just in case."

Sara spent the next half an hour going over the usual questions connected with the early stages of an investigation, asking Yvonne if the marriage was okay. Did Paul ever fall out with people? If so, who? What about their past, where they used to live? Did they leave the area under a cloud? Could she think of anyone with a reason who would want her husband dead?

But Yvonne sat there dazed, simply answering yes or no and very little else.

The doorbell rang around forty-five minutes later. Carla went to answer it, and a woman in her early fifties barged into the room and pulled Yvonne to her feet. That's when the dam really burst open.

"You must be Janice?" Sara asked. The two women were of similar height and weight, and both had the same facial features and hair colour.

"I am. Are you the officer I spoke to earlier?"

"That's correct. DI Sara Ramsey. We're about done here, unless there is anything you'd like to add, Yvonne?"

The sisters separated and sat beside each other on the couch, hands clasped tightly.

"I can't think of anything. My head is spinning like a tornado."

"That's understandable in the circumstances. I'm going to leave you one of my cards. If you think of anything later, don't hesitate to get in touch with me."

"Is that it?" Janice said. "Now what? You're just going to walk out and leave my sister to deal with this herself?"

"No, not at all. We need to get the investigation underway as quickly as possible. That's why I rang you to come and sit with your sister."

"It's okay, Janice. I'd rather it was you and me, anyway."

Janice glared at Sara. "I'm sorry, but I think it's wrong. Her husband has been killed, and you come in here, ask dozens of probably inept questions, and then flee from the scene within an hour or so of arriving. What's she supposed to do now? Brush herself down and get on with her life, is that it?"

Sara sighed inwardly. In the fifteen years she'd been on the Force, she was fortunate to have only been verbally attacked in this way a handful of times by a relative, and, each time, the victim's other half had stuck up for her, just like Yvonne had. "We can stay here for as long as Yvonne needs us, but that won't capture the person responsible for taking her husband's life, will it?"

Janice bowed her head. "I guess not. I'm sorry for my outburst. I think seeing all the forensic people outside kind of brought it home to me, you know, what we're dealing with here. It's bad enough being told over the phone what's happened, but seeing it for yourself is another matter entirely. Yes, you go, I'm here. I'll take care of Yvonne and Danny. Where is he?"

Yvonne sniffled and replied, "Probably upstairs in his room. I was too harsh on him. He was only trying to help, but he pressed the wrong buttons, and I let rip. I think he's forgiven me after our cuddle, but you know how quickly his mood can change."

"Only too well. Let's spend some time together first and then give him a shout in ten minutes or so. Will you still be around then?" Janice asked Sara.

"Possibly, we're going to have a chat with the pathologist, and see if she's stumbled across any clues yet, before we start knocking on the neighbours' doors to see if they saw anything last night."

"I doubt if they will have heard anything, not if it was lashing down last night," Janice said.

"That's probably true. Okay, ladies, give me a call if you need anything. We'll be in touch if we need clarification on anything during the investigation."

"I'll show you to the door." Janice jumped out of her seat before Sara could stop her.

At the front door, Janice held it open for them and lowered her voice to say, "Please, Paul was a good man. Don't let the killer get away with this. Yvonne and Danny deserve justice for his death."

"We're aware of that. I want to assure you we'll be doing our utmost to find the killer. Thank you for coming over to be with Yvonne. Take care of your sister and Danny."

"Don't worry, I will. Thank you for calling me. Good luck. I'm sorry if I appeared rude before."

"You didn't. It's forgotten about."

She closed the door as they walked down the steps towards the marquee. "I don't want to get too close and waste another suit. What did you make of the son issue?"

"Hard to tell. I suppose we'd need to know more about the disorder and how it's likely to affect someone's day-to-day life."

"From what I know about it, which I must admit is very little, I think there is quite a range of different ways it can affect a person. But yes, I agree, we should get someone on it right away."

"Want me to make the call?"

Sara nodded. "I'll see how things are progressing with Lorraine." She took a few steps forward, to the edge of the cordon, and called out to the pathologist, "Lorraine, are you there? Can you spare me a minute or two?"

Lorraine exited the marquee and crossed the gravel to meet her. "How did you get on in there?"

"Okay. The wife couldn't tell us much, only that he'd had a meeting with the residents at the church last night to discuss the Christmas events coming up."

"And the son? What were your thoughts about him?"

"Ah, at first, he seemed okay with us, but then things got bad between him and his mother, and she ended up telling him to leave the room. It wasn't until he'd left that his mother explained he is bipolar, plus he has ADHD."

"Ah, right, that explains the reaction we received when we arrived. His father's death is going to hit him hard, something for you to be aware of going forward, Sara."

"Thanks for the warning. We'll bear it in mind. Yvonne's sister has arrived from Worcester, leaving us to get on with the house-to-house enquiries. I just wondered if you had anything else for me before I head off."

"Not really, nothing new. Hopefully, the PM will shed more light on things. Do you want to attend this afternoon?"

"What the fuck are you doing down there? You should be getting on with the investigation instead of standing around gossiping," a male voice shouted from the house.

"Shit, it's the son. Let's hope he doesn't come out here and make a scene."

A woman's voice shouted inside the house, and Danny slammed his bedroom window shut.

"That told us," Lorraine said. "Are you coming this afternoon or not?"

"What time?"

"Around two, I can give you a proper time later."

"Yes, we'll be there, unless anything major crops up in the meantime."

"Good. I'm still struggling to get my head around why someone would kill a member of the clergy. It's sickening to think someone would have that much anger in them to go down that route. The wound to his stomach would have been enough to have killed him, given time."

"Hard to know what goes through a killer's mind at the best of times. Do you think we're looking for one perpetrator or a couple?"

"That's the question I'd love to know the answer to myself, but with no evidence to hand, I'm not sure if we're ever going to learn the truth."

"Christ, don't say that. At least give me something to hang on to. Right, we're going to get the show on the road. We'll be at your gaff at around two. Let me know if it's going to be later than that."

"I will. Good luck. I sense you're going to need a good dose of that to crack this case."

"Ever the optimist, eh?"

Lorraine grinned and walked back to the marquee. Sara joined Carla, who was in the process of tucking her phone into her pocket.

"All done?"

"Yes, I've got Marissa on the case. I thought we'd get more information if a woman did the research."

"Yikes, don't let the fellas on the team hear you say that."

Carla cringed. "I wasn't… meaning, anything bad… oh shit, really? Is that how it came across?"

"I'm teasing you. Stop being so gullible. Have you spotted any uniformed officers around?"

"There's a car up the road."

"We'll check in with them first and then come back here to question the immediate neighbours."

"After you." Carla made a sweeping gesture with her arm.

"Did you hear the commotion earlier while I was talking to Lorraine?"

"My eyesight might be a bit dodgy, but there's nothing wrong with my hearing. I sense we're going to need to tread carefully where laddo is concerned."

"I wholeheartedly agree. Lord knows how Yvonne is going to cope with him in the days or months ahead."

"I feel for her, what with having to contend with the loss of her husband as well."

"Yep, it's not going to be easy. Let's get our arses into gear and see what our colleagues have to say."

The two young officers finished talking to the residents they were dealing with and joined Sara and Carla at the patrol car.

"Hi, how's it going?" Sara asked.

"Not good so far, ma'am," the first officer said, and the second one concurred.

"Why am I not surprised, given the weather conditions last night? Okay, you carry on with the neighbours at this end of the village, and we'll make a start with the ones on either side of the vicarage and opposite it. We'll compare notes in an hour or so. How's that?"

Both officers nodded, and the four of them split up.

"I've got a sinking feeling about this case already," Carla grumbled.

"Me, too, although I'm trying hard to dismiss it. You go left, and I'll take the house on the right."

"Fair enough."

CHAPTER 2

*S*ara walked up the path to the nearest house and rang the doorbell. A woman with greying hair using a walking stick opened the door to the small cottage.

Sara flashed her warrant card and introduced herself to the woman. "Hello, sorry to trouble you. I'm DI Sara Ramsey from West Mercia Police. Do you have time for a quick chat?"

"Is this about what's gone on next door?"

"That's right."

"Yes, okay. Do you want to come in? I'm not too good on my feet these days and struggle to stand for any length of time."

"Of course, if that's what you prefer."

The woman backed up and turned awkwardly into the tight space by the stairs. "I'm sorry to hold you up. My advice would be to never get old, dear. It's a pain in the rear."

"I'm sorry to see you suffering like this. Can I help?"

"You can open the door for me. I'm hoping it's tidy in there. I don't get many visitors these days."

"That's a shame. Here, let me squeeze past you."

"I'm Helen, by the way."

"Have you lived here long, Helen?"

"All my life, well, in the village. I've only owned this house for twenty years, though. Regret having it now, I should have thought ahead and bought a bungalow instead, for obvious reasons."

Sara peered over her shoulder at the stairs and saw the stairlift. "Doesn't the lift help you?"

"When it's working. I've rung the company a dozen times or more since it broke down last week; they don't want to know, not when they've had the money out of you to fit it."

"That's so wrong. Do you want me to call them for you?"

She lowered herself into what appeared to be a comfy armchair and smiled. "Would you? My family doesn't care. They keep pestering me to go in a care home just so they can get their hands on this place, sell it off and take the proceeds, bloody idiots. Who the hell do they think will pay for my care if I do what they want?"

"Getting old brings out the worst in people, doesn't it?"

"You're not wrong. Still, that's my problem. I didn't mean to burden you with such nonsense."

"It's no bother. Let me call the company, give them a rocket up the arse, and then we'll have a chat. How's that?"

"That's so sweet of you. Can I get you a drink?"

"Not for me, thanks. I've not long had one next door with Mrs Gains."

"Terrible, terrible situation. I've been keeping an eye on things out of the side window. Oops, maybe I shouldn't have said that."

"It must be intriguing to have a crime scene on your doorstep."

"Never happened before. It's a terrible blow to the

community. My phone hasn't stopped ringing today. We're very close. I know the vicar and his wife have only lived here ten years or so, but we all welcomed him and his family. He'll be missed. I couldn't make it to the church, not that often, but I did my best. He appreciated that and would often drop by and see me if I hadn't attended, just to see how I was doing. Nice man. His wife always stops to say hello if I'm watering the plants in the garden."

"And what about the son?"

"Danny, I think he's called. I know he has an illness, but he's always been kind to me, so I won't have anything said against him."

"Has someone tried to run him down to you?"

"Often. I find people these days have less tolerance for those who are different."

"Ah, yes, I think you're right. Let me call the company, and we'll finish our conversation. Have you got the number?"

"On the table there, next to the phone."

"I'll use my mobile." Sara rang and spoke to the company's customer service advisor. "Yes, I'm Detective Inspector Sara Ramsey from the West Mercia Police. I've been called out to an address out in Wilton where I have found a very distressed lady who has been trying to get her stairlift fixed by your company for over a week. Can you tell me why you are failing in your duties to deal with this lady's request to get a technician out to repair one of your products?"

"I... umm... yes, I'm aware Mrs Rogers has rung us a couple of times. I've told her that due to staff shortages, there is a waiting list. I'd be happy to put her on that list, if she wants me to."

"And how long is it going to take before her name gets to the top?"

"Umm... possibly about four weeks."

"That's not good enough. I demand to speak to your manager."

"No, let me try to sort this out for you while you're on the phone. Please give me the opportunity to put things right."

"I'm waiting. This poor lady is disabled, and because of your lack of compassion and understanding, she's being forced to sleep on her couch every night. It's not good enough. I insist you sort Mrs Rogers out today. Otherwise, I will be forced to put in a complaint about your company through Trading Standards. Am I making myself clear?"

"Yes, very clear. I'm going to check if a technician is close to Mrs Rogers' house now. Please hold the line."

Sara winked at Helen and covered the mouthpiece of her mobile. "She's trying to get it sorted now."

"It's shocking that it should come to this, isn't it?"

Sara agreed. "Appalling. There's nothing I like more than to go into battle with a firm that treats their older customers disrespectfully."

"Hello, are you still there?" the young woman asked.

"I assure you, I'm not going anywhere until this problem has been dealt with."

"Yes, it will be, I promise you. I have a technician calling at a property in the village this afternoon. I can ask him to make an extra stop and visit Mrs Rogers, if that helps?"

"Will the problem with her stairlift be fixed today?"

"I can't promise that."

"I beg your pardon. For a moment there, I thought you said you weren't going to make the repairs today."

"If Pete can do it, then he will."

"Good, we'll expect to see him at what time?"

"Four-thirty, maybe sooner."

"Great stuff. Now, I want you to put on Mrs Rogers' file that if your equipment breaks down again, she should go to the top of the list, as a priority, to have it repaired. Am I making myself clear here?"

"Very clear. I'll do that now. Thank you for calling."

"Goodbye." Sara ended the call and punched the air. "Sorry, I shouldn't have done that, but I hate the thought of someone in your situation being treated with disrespect."

Helen's eyes teared up. "Oh, my goodness, that was amazing! Your parents must be so proud of you."

"Dad is, yes. Mum sadly passed away a couple of years ago. I miss her dearly, but life goes on, doesn't it?"

"It certainly does. I thought my life had ended when my Bert left me, but I coped. I'm still coping."

"You're doing amazingly well. How many children do you have?"

"Three, two girls and a boy. All in their forties now with kids of their own. Don't ask me how many grandchildren I have. I lost count after ten, or was it twelve?"

Sara laughed. "Oops. It can't be easy, keeping count."

"It's not. But you're not here to talk about me and my offspring."

"It would be good to speak with you about what happened last night. Did you either see or hear anything?"

"No, I wish I had. Although when I opened my bedroom curtains this morning, what I saw, will remain with me until my dying day. My legs gave way beneath me. I tried to get up for over half an hour. Finally, I summoned up the strength from somewhere. Lord knows how or where."

"I'm sorry you had to witness that; it must have been horrific for you. I'm glad you found the strength to get on your feet. How did you get upstairs, with your stairlift being out of action?"

"Don't laugh, but I crawled up on my hands and knees. I couldn't bring myself to sleep down here. That couch is so lumpy."

"I think it's sad your family doesn't care enough to come and see you. Would you like me to call them?"

Helen sniggered behind her hand. "You forget I've seen you in action. If you spoke to any of my kids that way, they'd never set foot in this house again."

"I wasn't that bad, was I?"

"No comment."

Sara laughed. She felt an affinity with this old lady who reminded her of her grandmother, whom she used to be close to in her teens, after her grandfather had passed away. Sara had stepped up to the plate for her family, unlike Helen's.

"I know the weather was against us last night, but did you hear anything? Perhaps a car pulled up outside your property?"

"No, nothing at all. My hearing isn't the best these days. I went to bed at around ten, and the first thing I do is take my hearing aid out and put it on the bedside table, along with my false teeth." She laughed. "I can tell that was too much information."

Sara held her finger and thumb half an inch apart. "Just a little."

"I really don't have any information for you. I'm sorry."

"It's okay. It was a long shot, anyway. Don't feel as though you've let us or the family down."

"I do, though. Will I be safe here by myself tonight? What if this person is out there, watching the proceedings today, the aftermath of what they did to our vicar? And he or she sees you leaving my house. What then?"

"I'm going to give you one of my cards. Any problems, I want you to call nine-nine-nine first and then me. Do you hear me?"

"I do. I won't be putting you to any trouble like that, dear.

You have enough to deal with as it is. I'll be fine, hopefully. You must admit it's worrying, though."

"I don't want you to worry. My intention is to have a couple of police cars patrolling the area tonight, actually, for the next few nights. I'm sure you won't be the only resident concerned about their safety."

"That would be amazing. We can't thank you enough for thinking about us."

"It's what we're here for, to keep the general public safe in the eye of the storm. I'm going to leave you to it now. Is there anything I can do for you before I go?"

"I don't think so. You've been very kind."

"Why don't I bring your mattress downstairs for you?"

Helen smiled. "I'm all right. Don't worry about me. I'll get down on my hands and knees again and take my time going upstairs."

"I could drop back later to help you. I hate to think of you struggling unnecessarily."

"Honestly, you don't need to worry about me, but if it will put your mind at ease, I'll call you if I have a problem."

"I hope you do. Stay there. I can see myself out."

"Where are you going to go next?"

Sara stood and walked towards the door. The large house across the road caught her eye. "I'm leaning towards knocking on the neighbour opposite. I don't suppose you know their name, do you?"

"Yes, they're Zoe and Josh. They only bought the property last year. Nice couple. I don't think they're short of a bob or two, judging by the luxury cars they both drive."

"An Audi is sitting in the drive now. Does that belong to the wife or the husband?"

"What colour is it?"

"Red."

"That's Zoe's. Sometimes she works from home. I hope she can be of more use to you than I've been."

"Fingers crossed. Take care of yourself."

"Thinking about it, I'd better come and put the safety chain on the door. It's at times like this, I wish I still had a dog. Even a yapper can act as a deterrent."

"Might be an idea. They're brilliant company for people living alone, too."

"I'll give it some serious consideration. The only problem with that is that I wouldn't be able to take it out for a walk. It wouldn't be fair to it."

"Depends on what type of dog you get. Bye for now."

Sara waved at Helen as she shut the garden gate. She walked past the vicarage and noticed Lorraine and her team were packing up, getting ready to leave the crime scene. Carla was still standing on the doorstep of the other neighbour's house. Sara lingered by the gate for a few minutes until her partner finished interviewing the homeowner.

"Sorry, I didn't see you there. Everything all right?"

"Fine. I wanted to see if you'd had any success before I moved on to the next one."

"Not really. What about you?"

"Nothing, although I carried out my good deed for the day."

Carla frowned. "And what was that?"

"A lady called Helen, her stairlift had broken down, and she was having trouble getting the company to come out to repair it."

"So, Superhero Sara came to the rescue, right?"

Sara's face heated up. "Kind of. I threatened the woman on the phone with Trading Standards if she didn't send a technician out ASAP."

"Don't tell me that worked."

"It did. She's sending someone out this afternoon to fix it."

"Great result. I bet... Helen, was it?"

Sara nodded.

"I bet she was grateful for your interference... I mean, your kind intervention."

Sara slapped Carla's arm. "Cheeky cow. She was extremely grateful, if you must know. Nice lady. She had the shock of her life first thing."

"Did she see someone next door at the vicarage?"

"No, she saw the vicar's body hanging from the tree."

"Ouch, I'm surprised she didn't have a heart attack if she's that frail."

"Her body might let her down occasionally, but I think she's got a strong will and determination, which makes up for it."

"Did she see anything last night, around the time of the murder?"

"No, nothing at all. I think our next step should be to go over the road, see what the residents opposite the vicarage saw."

"Sounds good. You go left and I'll go right."

They crossed the road, and Sara entered the driveway of Zoe's house. She rang the bell, and instead of the homeowner coming to the door, she spoke to Sara through the doorbell camera.

"Hello, can I help you?"

Sara showed her ID to the camera. "I'm DI Sara Ramsey. I was hoping to have a quick word with you, if you have the time."

"Regarding what?"

"Are you at home? It would be easier to speak with you in person."

"I'll come down. Come in when you hear the buzzer."

Sara jumped slightly when the buzzer sounded. It was louder than she'd expected it would be. She entered the porch of the home and opened the inner door. A woman in her mid-thirties, wearing a smart pair of black trousers and a cream blouse, descended the stairs ahead of her. She held out her hand to shake once she'd reached the bottom.

"I'm Zoe. Does this have anything to do with what's going on over the road at the vicarage?"

"Yes, I was wondering if you either heard or saw anything last night."

"No, neither of us did. However, when my husband left this morning, he saw the vicar... and came to get me. I tore down the stairs to have a look; neither of us could believe it. We didn't call the police because we saw Yvonne out there. She was kneeling below her husband; I presumed she was praying."

"It's an horrendous situation for the family to deal with."

"And the community. He was a lovely man, too young and too nice to die like that. He didn't do it himself, did he? That was my first thought before Josh told me not to be so ridiculous."

"No, we don't believe that to be the case at all."

"Yeah, I suppose he would have chosen a better night to have committed suicide, wouldn't he? Last night was the pits. So, what do you suspect happened to him? And why did the murderer choose to do it when the weather was so bad?"

"Hopefully, that will become clear during our investigation. I fear it's going to prove difficult, though." A sudden thought hit her. She turned and glanced across the street through the glass inner door. "Wait a second, the doorbell camera. You saw I was standing on the doorstep, right?"

"I did. Oh shit, you don't think...?"

"Would you be willing to have a look through the footage for me?"

53

"It's quite new. Josh only installed it a few months ago. I think I saw the instruction booklet in a drawer in the kitchen. Come through, I'll see if I can find it."

She sped through the hallway, and Sara followed close behind her, her adrenaline pumping at the prospect of finally finding a snippet of evidence they could latch on to at last.

"There's only one place it can be. I was looking for the shopping pad to make a list of what we need from the supermarket the other day, and I'm sure I pushed the instructions to one side." Zoe opened the drawer and squealed. "Yes, it's here."

Sara smiled at the excited woman. "That's brilliant news. Is there any way we can view the footage now? Maybe it picked up what happened."

"Of course. It might take me a few minutes to sort through it. I'm not very technically minded, are you?"

"I've had my moments over the years, but not if the device is too technical."

"I need to find my specs first; I've left them upstairs. I'll be back in a tick."

Sara took the opportunity to give Carla a quick call. "Sorry to interrupt, I think I've found something. Is it convenient for you to join me?"

"On my way. I'd finished at the house next door and was moving on to the next one. I'll double back and be with you shortly."

"I'll come and open the door for you." She stepped back into the hallway as Zoe came thundering down the stairs.

"What? You're not going, are you?"

"No, I hope it's all right, I've asked my partner to join us."

"Go for it. The more heads, the better. Would you like a drink?"

"No, we don't want to put you to any bother."

"You won't be. I'll make a pot of coffee. I could do with

some caffeine running through my veins, especially when reading instructions. They tend to test everyone's will to live, don't they? Damn, perhaps that was a touch insensitive, given the situation."

"Don't worry, I thought nothing of it. You're allowed to have a slip of the tongue sometimes."

The doorbell rang.

"Shall I get that? It'll probably be my partner."

"Yes, you do that while I make the drinks. How do you take yours?"

"Both white with one sugar, thank you." Sara opened the front door. "Hi, come in."

"What's going on?"

"There's a doorbell camera on the front door."

"I noticed it. Yes, that could be good," Carla said, the penny dropping.

"Let's hope so. It's not like we have anything else to go on as yet. Zoe is making us a coffee. She's dug out the instructions. We're going to go through them together. I don't suppose you have an idea how they work, do you?"

Carla's mouth hitched up at one side. "Are you kidding me? No way. I steer clear of setting things up like a new TV in our house. Even when I was single, I used to get my dad over to do it for me."

"Sounds about right," Sara said. "I think I did the same with mine before Mark came along." She picked up the small booklet and flicked through it. "Ah, it says here that it comes with an SD card."

"Ah, yes, that's right. That's not always the case. I think Josh chose that one specifically because it had backup potential that wasn't only online."

"Now all we have to do is locate it."

Zoe placed three mugs on the island in front of them and then held out her hand for the instructions. "May I?"

Sara handed it over and then moved to stand alongside her so that they could both view the booklet at the same time. Zoe annoyingly flicked through the pages swiftly. Sara gave up and had her coffee instead.

Moments later, frustration got the better of Zoe, and she threw the instructions on the counter. "Damn thing, none of it makes sense to me. Maybe I should give Josh a call."

"Let me have a quick look first. If all else fails, then you can ring your husband."

"If you insist. Maybe that's a trait of mine. I give up too easily and find myself being more and more reliant on my husband. Strange how we go from being confident women to not giving two hoots and allowing our husbands to take over once a ring is put on our finger, isn't it?"

Sara hated to agree with her. However, that's exactly how things were at home with Mark. She chuckled and whispered, "No comment."

Carla cleared her throat. "Yeah, you can leave me out of this conversation, too."

Sara jabbed a thumb in Carla's direction. "Newlywed in our midst."

"How wonderful. How long?"

"Now you're asking... three, or is it four months now? Time flies when you're having fun, apparently," Carla added the quip to cover her back.

Sara laughed. "It's actually nearer to six months."

Carla put a hand over her mouth and then dropped it. "Oops. Silly me."

Sara flicked to the back of the booklet. "Ah, what's this? Can I take it with me, to match the diagram to the equipment?" She showed Zoe the image she had found. "The card should be at the side."

"By all means. You've got more patience than me for reading those damn things."

Sara left the kitchen and compared the image to the doorbell camera. She removed a small cover on the right-hand side, and there it was, the SD card. "I've found it. Would it be all right to take it out?"

"Yes, of course," Zoe responded.

Sara's heart raced, and she removed the miniature card and marched back to the kitchen with it.

"That's bloody tiny," Carla said.

"You're not wrong. I hope we don't lose it on the way to the lab."

"I've got a bag in my pocket." Carla withdrew a plastic bag and offered it to Sara.

"Has it been used?"

"Honestly? I can't remember."

"I've got a roll of new ones, if you'd prefer," Zoe offered.

"Maybe that would be for the best, thanks."

Zoe opened another drawer and removed a roll of bags. After tearing one off and giving it to Sara, she said, "Don't you want to view it first before you leave?"

"Do you have a laptop handy?"

"I can bring it down from upstairs. It's in my office."

"That would be helpful, thank you."

Zoe left the room. Moments later, footsteps sounded overhead, and, not long after, she thundered back down the stairs to join them again. She flipped the lid open, and the computer sprang to life. "I never shut it down properly. Nuts, I know."

"I'm the same with mine," Carla admitted.

Zoe inserted the card into the slot and went through the motions of searching for the right day on the menu. "Ah, here it is. You can see how bad the rain was. It was torrential on and off from around eight, I believe."

She scrolled through the timeline and then paused the

footage when a figure came into view carrying an umbrella. "That's Paul. Looks like he's in a hurry."

"You have quite an angle on the camera, I'm guessing, to cover your drive. Wait, what's this?"

A car came to a stop beside the vicar. The passenger car door smashed into Paul's leg. A figure dressed in black got out of the passenger seat and approached him. He moved closer, and they talked for a few moments, then the passenger lashed out with his fists. Paul stumbled backwards into the hedge. He dropped his umbrella and held up his hands, obviously pleading with the person to stop hitting him. Then the passenger pulled something out of his jacket.

"Jesus, that's when he must have been stabbed," Sara mumbled.

"Oh no, I didn't know Paul was stabbed first."

Sara cringed. "I'm going to need you to keep quiet about what you witness here, Zoe."

"I will, I promise. The person just did it, off the cuff. Do you think they knew Paul? Do you think he did something earlier to provoke the attack?"

"Possibly. The investigation has only just begun, and this is the first piece of evidence to come our way."

"Who'd have thought it? Because of the rain, the image isn't that clear, but it's still good enough to show us what happened. Poor Paul, I can't believe my eyes."

They watched on in silence as Paul put a hand over his midriff, then he staggered backwards towards the hedge again after his leg gave way. He was pulled to his feet again, and the passenger shoved him in the back. Paul hobbled towards home and received another shove in the back. They walked through the gates of the vicarage. They talked before the wall obscured the view slightly. Then the driver joined them. "Bugger, that's not good. Can we fast-forward it a little?"

Zoe pressed a button on her computer and played it until the smaller of the two people, the driver, reappeared and rushed back to the car. The person removed a bag from the boot and returned to the crime scene.

"I'm guessing the ropes were in the bag," Sara muttered.

"Ropes? They used more than one?" Zoe glanced her way to ask.

"Yes, his feet and hands were tied together as well."

"Shocking. Was this intentional? Why would they be carrying ropes, more to the point, a noose, in the boot of their car?"

"Precisely. We believe it was planned. It had to have been, taking into consideration the equipment they used. It has confirmed one thing we weren't sure about."

"There were two killers, not just one," Carla whispered, her gaze still fixed on the screen.

"Correct," Sara replied. "Also, they came dressed for the occasion, so yes, I'm inclined to believe the attack was definitely premeditated. The question is, why? Everyone we've spoken to so far has told us that Paul was a really nice man."

"He is—sorry, he was. Paul always got involved in the community. He sat on the parish council as well, not sure how many vicars would do that, are you?"

"Not heard of that at all, shows his commitment to the residents. Can you press Play again and we'll see what happens next?"

Zoe did just that, and they stared at the wall for what seemed like an age until she whizzed it forward again. The two people bolted out of the grounds of the vicarage and jumped in the car.

"It would be great if we could get a number plate for the vehicle," Sara said.

"I'll slow it down, see what shows up."

They watched on, their breaths held.

"There, I can make it out," Carla said. She removed her notebook and scribbled down the registration number.

Sara patted Zoe on the shoulder. "This is brilliant news. We can't thank you enough for this, Zoe. Maybe gadgets like this do have a place in our world after all."

"I should say so. I'm glad it's been of use to you. Take the card, it came with a second one. I'll slot that in after you leave, and we should be good to go again."

"We'll get this one back to you ASAP. The lab will probably make a copy."

"No rush. You do what you have to do. Before you go, can I ask how Yvonne and Danny are today?"

Sara sighed. "As you can imagine, they're both very shaken up by the events. Yvonne's sister, Janice, has just arrived from Worcester to be with them."

"I'm glad another relative has come to be with them. It wouldn't be right for them to be alone in that vast, rambling house. It seems so sinister and uninviting. When we first moved here, I must admit it caused me to shudder on more than one occasion."

"That's the problem with some buildings dating back centuries, they were often built to look austere."

"Yes, perhaps that's it. What will the family do now?"

Shrugging, Sara said, "Hard to know at this early stage. I suppose they'll be asked to pack up and leave once a new vicar has been chosen for the parish."

"Oh dear, that seems a shame to get tossed out of your home, especially in the circumstances. The trouble is, none of us know what's around the corner, do we?"

"Indeed. Which is why we should live life to the fullest, every day."

"Oh, yes, I couldn't have said it better myself. We've recently lost my father, and I've pretty much said the same to my mum. She's still dealing with the immense grief, but once she's got hold of that, I've told her she should withdraw some of her savings and take off somewhere. Maybe a cruise around the Med or the Caribbean would suit her. It was something they'd been planning to do for a while before Dad was struck down with dementia. Such a terrible disease that scientists need to find a way of eradicating. It's been with us for decades now, and they don't seem to be making any headway with it." She wiped away a tear that had slipped from her right eye. "I'm sorry. I still get emotional when I think about him. The last six weeks of his life were the worst I've ever had to encounter; it was a darn sight worse for Mum. Not sure how she coped, but she did. We all did. We showed a rallying spirit to keep Dad going, but the disease…"

Sara rubbed her arm. "I'm sorry you and your family had to go through that and, I'm with you, a lot more should be done to combat the terrible disease."

"The days are getting easier. I promised my husband I wouldn't dwell on it."

"Sometimes that's easier said than done, though, isn't it?"

"It sure is. Anyway, will you pass on my condolences to the Gainses? Tell them if they need anything, I'm sure the community will rally around should they need us."

"I'll pass that on and thank you for helping us out today with the footage."

"I just hope it leads you to the killers. They need to be caught and put in prison for life for taking our vicar from us."

"We're going to do our very best to ensure that happens."

Sara and Carla left the house and crossed the road to the vicarage. Lorraine was putting her large medical bag in the back of her van. She'd removed her protective suit, so they knew it was okay to approach her.

"Are you off now?" Sara asked.

"Yep, the techs are just finishing up. The body is on the

way to the mortuary, and I've said farewell to Yvonne and her sister."

"How were they?"

"As I would expect, after all they've been through. What about you? You look different." Lorraine narrowed her eyes and inclined her head. "As if you've stumbled across some interesting evidence, am I right?"

"We have. It turns out the woman living in the house opposite has one of those doorbell cameras."

Lorraine's eyes widened. "And it caught the murder. Is that what you're telling me?"

"Sort of. I mean, it would have if that brick wall hadn't been in the way. However, what it did show was that a car drew up. Initially, one person got out of the vehicle and attacked Paul, then pulled a knife on him. That person slit the victim's stomach open. Paul Gains held a hand over his stomach. They then shoved the vicar through the gates and into the garden. Then the accomplice got out of the vehicle and went to the boot; they must have, presumably, removed the ropes."

Lorraine stared at her, shaking her head. "What the actual fuck?"

"Hard to believe. The good news is that we caught the number plate of the vehicle. We're on our way back to the station via the lab. We've got the SD card from the camera. I was hoping Forensics would be able to do their stuff and get a close-up of the two perpetrators."

"Great call. I'll have a word. Get them to make it a priority."

"That's what I was hoping you'd say."

"Well, what are you waiting for? You'd better get a move on if you're going to attend the PM at two."

"Damn, I forgot all about that. We'll be there."

"Don't be late," Lorraine shouted after them as they ran back to the car.

"I thought you might drop in to see Yvonne before we leave," Carla queried.

Sara unlocked the car and slid behind the steering wheel. "I don't think I could face it. Let's see what transpires with the car first. I'd feel bad telling her about it only for it to be a false alarm."

Carla clicked her seat belt in place. "I doubt if that's going to be the case. Want me to ring the team, get them doing the necessary, or would you rather we do it ourselves?"

"No, why waste time? Yes, ring them. I'll drive to the lab; hopefully, they'll have some news for us by the time we get back in the car."

Carla made the call and gave the task of hunting down the registration of the vehicle to Barry, who promised to have a response for them soon.

Sara parked outside the lab. "I won't be long. You might as well stay here." When she entered, a tech was coming out of one of the offices. "Sorry to trouble you. Can someone deal with this for me? I've run it past Lorraine, and she told me she'd put a top-priority notice on it."

The tech peered at the plastic bag she was holding up. "Is that an SD card?"

"That's right. It's got crucial evidence of a murder scene. Who shall I see about dealing with it?"

"I'll handle it. Leave it with me. Is this the murder at the vicarage?"

"Correct. There were two suspects in the footage. We need their photos enhanced. We're also running the plates for their vehicle as well."

"Glad something good has come of it already."

"Believe me, so am I. How soon can I expect a result?"

"A couple of days. I'm clear at the moment, and yes, I'll make it my priority to get back to you."

"That's great. What's your name?"

"Terry Vowels."

"Well, Terry, good luck with your task."

"Ha, let's hope the card doesn't self-destruct before I have time to view it."

"Don't even joke about things like that. I'll leave you my card, ring me as soon as you have anything of use."

"I will. It's in safe hands, don't worry."

"Thanks." She left via the exit and returned to her vehicle.

"How did it go?" Carla asked.

"Fine. How about you? Has Barry got back to you yet?"

"Yes, just. It's not good news."

Sara closed her eyes and groaned. "Don't tell me, the car was stolen."

"All right then, I won't, but it was."

Sara resisted the temptation to take her frustration out on the steering wheel for a change and got out of the car again. Once she was outside, she opened her lungs and screamed. Feeling better, she got back in the car and stared at her bemused partner. "Something wrong?"

Carla pulled a face. "I was about to ask you that very question. What the hell was that all about?"

"The last time I vented my frustration on the steering wheel, I hurt the heel of my hand, so I thought I'd mix things up a bit. Shouting outside the car was a far more practical thing to do, don't you agree?"

"I might have, if I'd been warned you were going to do it."

"Do I have to inform you about my every move during the day?"

Carla crossed her arms and stared out of the side window. "All right, snarky knickers."

"Is that any way to address a senior officer?" Sara said, doing her best to suppress the giggle tickling her throat.

"Are you for real?"

"No, I'm teasing. I'm sensing everything isn't as it should be with you. Are you going to tell me what's wrong?"

"I'm fine, eager to get on with solving the case. It really isn't sitting well with me that, in a small community like this, someone should choose the vicar to kill."

Sara started the engine and pulled into the flow of traffic after a kind motorist let her out. "It's not like you to get so upset about an investigation. Are you sure there's nothing else going on?"

"No, I'm sure. It's the frustration that's bugging the hell out of me. Seeing the footage of the car, I couldn't help but get excited at the prospect of wrapping the case up early and banging the perpetrators in a cell where they belong. Now we're scuppered before we've even had the opportunity to put a plan into action."

"Shit happens. You know that as well as I do, Carla. Don't let it get you down. Things will soon overwhelm you if you do. You know how things like this work."

"You're right. I know I'm being silly. Why can't a case be simple and just slot into place easily for a change? Why do we always have to go the long way around, especially when we've got the evidence to prove who killed the victim?"

"It's called life. Are you sure there's nothing else bothering you?"

"No, there isn't," Carla snapped back.

Her feistiness set alarm bells ringing for Sara. She accepted the warning and left things as they stood, for now, and completed the rest of the journey in silence.

·   ·   ·

After Sara and Carla attended the PM and returned to the station, the afternoon dragged by. The team, despite their best efforts in their absence, had failed to find anything bad in the news archives about the vicar, his wife, or his son. The car had been stolen from a car park in Hereford during the previous day. The owner of the vehicle hadn't logged the call with the police until eight p.m. because she had been on a trip with a friend. They'd caught the train together to Bristol to do some Christmas shopping. When the woman had returned, her car wasn't there, so her friend had insisted she take her to the police station to report the crime.

Sara's mood got worse when Terry Vowels rang from the lab to say he had enhanced the images of the suspects the best he could. The pictures were too grainy to be of much use. He'd sent the results through to Sara via email, and her frustration kicked up a notch when she delivered the news to her team.

"So where does that leave the investigation, then?" Carla asked, obviously still in a sour mood.

"It means that we have to dig deeper to find the killers. We've been here before, Carla. There's no need for us to give up, not this early in the proceedings."

"I wasn't suggesting we should. I was merely asking the question." Carla folded her arms tightly and slipped low in her chair.

Sara ignored her partner's childish behaviour, as if she didn't have enough to deal with at present. What with having the funeral of Mark's mother to attend within the next few days and all that entailed.

"Okay, let's call it a day and head home. Hopefully, casting fresh eyes over what little we've got so far might prove to be more beneficial to us in the morning."

"Wishful thinking," Carla mumbled, just loud enough for Sara to hear.

"Goodnight, folks. Thanks for all your efforts today. Carla, join me in my office for a quick chat, will you?"

Carla locked a defiant gaze with her. She reluctantly tucked her chair under her desk and flicked off her computer screen, then joined Sara in her office.

Sara had her fingers steepled together. "Come in. Take a seat."

"Is this where you give me a bollocking?"

"What's got into you the last few hours? You were all right when we first showed up at the crime scene. Now you're acting... well, it's not like me to say this but, well, like a bloody child."

Her partner shrugged and glanced down at her hands settled in her lap.

"I can't help you if you won't tell me what's wrong with you. Come on, spill."

"Nothing. I've told you, this case isn't sitting comfortably with me because of who the victim is."

"Do you know him personally?"

"No, of course I don't."

"Then why should it affect you like this?"

Carla remained silent, but Sara could tell she was searching for the right words to say. "I can't, it's too raw."

"What is? You can't leave me dangling like this, Carla. Why won't you open up to me? What am I missing here?"

Carla shook her head and attempted to leave her seat.

"You walk out of this office and there's no way back for you. I'll be forced to find another partner." Her double bluff failed.

"Then so be it, if that's what you truly want."

"I don't. Stop shutting me out, Carla. I thought we were friends."

Tears glistened in Carla's eyes. "We are. Don't pull that one on me. Why can't you leave things alone?"

"Because I care, that's why. You might not think I do, but it's the bloody truth. Please, why are you keeping secrets from me? This isn't going to go away by the look of it, so you might as well come right out and tell me. What's happened during the day to turn your mood on its head?"

"Nothing. Please, can we leave it there?"

Sara picked up a pen and threw it at the wall behind Carla. "Tell me, damn you! Does this have anything to do with Des? Your marriage? What's going on, mate?"

"Nothing, and you throwing things, exerting your power over me, is only going to make matters worse, not better."

"Me exerting my power over you? Since when have I ever done that?" Sara glared, holding Carla's gaze. "You know what? I give up, go home. And I hope, for your sake, you wake up in a better mood tomorrow."

"You, too." Carla left her seat and walked out of the office.

Sara sat there, seething for at least five minutes, her mind in turmoil, struggling to find out what had gone wrong during Carla's day to put her in such a foul mood. She switched off her computer and the office light and made her way down the stairs to her car. She stopped off at the supermarket to pick up a bottle of wine and a couple of steaks for dinner. En route, she rang Mark. "Hi, it's me. How was your day?"

"Fine, and yours?"

"Mixed, I'll tell you about it when I get home. Have you cooked anything?"

"No, I've not been home long myself. Why?"

"I've picked up some steaks and a bottle of wine."

"A mid-week bottle of wine? Should I be nervous?"

"No, I thought we could both do with it, especially tonight, with the daunting task lying ahead of us."

"If you're not up to it, I can postpone it for twenty-four hours."

"No, you can't. Your dad would have a fit. We're going over the arrangements to ease it for him, remember?"

"We are, you're right. How long are you going to be?"

"Around twenty minutes. You could peel some spuds or see if there is a bag of frozen chips in the freezer."

"Leave it with me. Drive safely."

"Don't worry, I will." She ended the call, and her thoughts automatically turned to Carla, so much so that she pulled over in the lay-by at the bottom of the steep hill that took her home and texted her partner.

SORRY IF I was off with you. I hope you have a good evening. Ring me later if you want to chat. Love, your friend, Sara.

SARA THREW the phone on the seat beside her, and it clattered against the bottle of wine she'd bought. "Ouch, good job I didn't break it. Wouldn't fancy mopping up red wine from the seat."

She arrived home to find Mark feeding their cat, Misty, in the kitchen. The cat ignored her, getting her priorities right.

Mark walked towards Sara and kissed her. She touched his face. "How have you been today?"

"Still a little weary, but I'm getting there. I should be able to open up the clinic fully by the end of next week."

He was recovering from cancer treatment, which had taken its toll on him over the past few months and, despite his best efforts to get back to work, his body was telling him he wasn't ready to cope with it full time, not yet.

"There's no need to rush back, especially if you're still feeling tired, love."

"I know, but going back will help take my mind off..." He paused and gulped. "What needs to be done towards the funeral?"

"Have you contacted your dad today?"

"Yes, he broke down again. I feel awful about not being there for him."

"You shouldn't. You ring him daily. He knows we both care about him."

"I know. I wish he'd take us up on our offer of coming for a visit."

"I can understand him not wanting to. We're both at work most of the day, and he'd be sitting here staring at the four walls. He should stay in familiar surroundings, don't you agree?"

"I do because you always talk a lot of sense. Anyway, let's get the dinner on the go. While we do that together, you can tell me how your day went."

She unloaded the carrier bag and said, "You first."

"It mostly comprised of being scratched by a couple of cats and being peed on by one or two puppies. All in a day's work."

"You're amazing, the way you brush it off, as if it's the most natural thing in the world to contend with."

"It is, for a vet. Do you want some broccoli and peas with this?"

"Anything that's to hand, don't worry too much."

"So, come on, tell me how your day was."

They prepared the vegetables together; at the same time, Sara went through what had happened at the vicarage.

"What the...? That's terrible. Fancy the wife finding her husband like that."

"Not the best start to her day, or anyone else's if they were confronted with the same scenario. I have a sense this case is going to test us to the limits as a team."

"Oh, why?"

"The location is against us, no cameras in the area, except the odd doorbell cam here and there, and a lot of good that's proved to be so far."

"By the sound of it, the criminals have a wealth of experience under their belts."

He'd hit on something they hadn't considered as a team. "You could be right; I'll get the team on it first thing."

"Glad to be of service. Fancy choosing a man of God to kill. That's not the done thing at all, is it? What's his background? Have you checked on that yet?"

"Nothing has shown up so far. His family moved to the area about ten years ago. The team has done its best, but has found no red flags in his background that would warrant someone wanting to murder him. It's the method they used that is bugging the hell out of me. Lorraine reckons the wound to his stomach would have been enough to have killed him, but no, the killers went on to hang him as well."

"The final act ensured his complete annihilation and any risk of survival. Do you think it's a one-off or was he specifically targeted?" Mark put the steaks in the pan with a knob of butter.

"We believe the murder was premeditated, judging by the equipment they took with them to the scene."

"Yes, sorry, I missed that. Some detective I would make, eh?"

Sara laughed and kissed him. "Hey, your expertise lies elsewhere. I couldn't perform surgery on Misty, if the need ever arose. I was utterly useless when that mongrel poisoned her, which led me to you sorting out my pussy for me."

He raised an eyebrow. "There's an answer to that, but I'm not going there."

"Yeah, best not to. We don't want to lower the tone of this conversation, do we?"

He sniggered. "You know me so well."

Sara put the chips in the air fryer and turned the gas burners on under the broccoli and the peas. "All this is in hand; can I run upstairs and get changed? I hate the smell of death lingering on me at the table when I'm trying to enjoy my meal."

"Yes, do it. Thanks for sharing that ghastly image with me as well."

"Sorry. Love you." She flew out of the kitchen and up the stairs, taking her phone with her. After changing out of her work suit and into her velour comfies, she checked her messages to see if Carla had responded. She hadn't. Sara sat on the edge of the bed and sent another quick text, asking if her friend and partner was okay. She knew Carla had read both messages, but she was still ignoring her.

Feeling down, she returned to the kitchen. Mark picked up on the fact there was something wrong when she turned her back on him to tend to the chips. He slipped his arms around her waist.

"Everything okay?" he whispered in her ear.

She faced him. "I'm not sure. Carla and I had a mini falling-out today. I've messaged her twice since we left, and she's giving me the cold shoulder."

He kissed the tip of her nose and squeezed her tightly. "Let things lie for now. I'm sure she'll come around soon, love."

"I hope so. I hate it when there's any kind of rift between us. It doesn't bode well, not when you're partners during an intense investigation."

"Then you're going to need to sit down with her in the morning and thrash it out."

"My sentiments exactly. I tried to do that before we clocked off this evening; she was having none of it, though."

"I'm sorry, you can do without the hassle at this time, Sara."

"I'm sure it's something and nothing. It'll blow over soon enough. I just wish she'd open up to me. I can't help to resolve the issue until she does. I wonder what triggered her reaction today. One minute she was fine, and the next, the shutters came down, and she just locked me out. We've been through some tough times together over the years. I was there when she reached her lowest ebb. I thought she was on firmer ground now since she married Des, but maybe there's something brewing there that she's shielding from me."

He kissed her and gave her another squeeze. "You're the best friend anyone could wish to have. Give her time, she'll come to realise that, eventually."

She hugged him, her thoughts still very much with Carla. She pulled away from Mark and checked the contents of the air fryer. "My part of the dinner is ready. How are the steaks coming along?"

"Damn, I forgot all about them." He sprinted over to the stove and flipped the steaks. "Umm… well, one of us is going to enjoy their meal tonight, and I don't think it's going to be me."

"Oh no. Sorry, that's my fault. Me being selfish again when we have bigger fish, or should that be steaks, to fry?"

"It'll be fine, I hope. We're ready to go. At least the vegetables are cooked to perfection."

Sara took on the responsibility of dishing up the meal while Mark opened the bottle of wine. All was right in her world with this man alongside her, or sitting opposite her, at the table. "To us and to what lies ahead of us in the days and months ahead."

"With you by my side, darling wife, there's only going to be one outcome, success."

They clinked their glasses together and tucked into their meal.

"It's not too bad, is it? Your steak?"

"Nope, actually it's perfect with added colour, still nice and juicy."

After dinner, they took the rest of their wine through to the lounge to discuss the arrangements for the funeral. Mark showed her how far his father had got; bless him, it wasn't far. He was floundering like a lost soul, missing his wife more than either of them realised.

"I hate to think of him all alone at a time like this," Sara said. She put the notebook aside and rested her head on Mark's chest. She found it comforting to hear his heart beating.

"Life goes on. He needs to learn to cope with his loss. I know that sounds harsh, but if he doesn't, then he's going to go downhill quickly. I can't lose him as well, Sara."

"We can't stop the inevitable from happening, but we can certainly delay it."

CHAPTER 3

◈

That night there was a public meeting being held at the community hall. The turnout was better than any of the residents could imagine, and that was either because of the important issue being raised, namely the disgusting smell and noise the residents had put up with for the two years since one of the farms in the village had been sold, or because of Paul Gains being killed the previous evening.

The residents who had been most affected by the smell and the level of noise coming from the farm at unsociable hours had been meeting at Natalie Everard's house for the past couple of months, since a planning application had gone in from the farmer Ralph Windsor. He'd taken over the farm, which at the time it went on the market only housed up to two hundred cattle, unlike what was going on there today. The community had learnt that Windsor was holding up to seven hundred cows on the site. The animals were forced to live in barns, never allowed to graze in the surrounding fields. It had become an intensive farming unit, where cattle were brought in weekly to fatten up quickly before being transported to the slaughterhouse.

That meant the number of waggons going in and out of the farm weekly had significantly increased. The farmer was crushing barley on site for the cattle feed. Because of the amount of cattle being housed, it meant the noisy feed machine was being used constantly throughout the day. Some residents had complained there was a fishy smell filling the local area from the food, as well as an unusual amount of harmful dust covering people's homes and cars. The nearby neighbours affected weren't able to put their washing on the line or even sit in their gardens during the day or in the evening. Their social lives impacted considerably.

It was the wrong environment to house a 'beef finishing unit' like this. In the centre of the community, it should have been more rural. As it was, homes surrounded the farm. The residents were requesting the business be relocated and were appalled to see yet another planning application had gone in to the council. This time, the farmer had erected a barn specifically to keep equipment. Ever since that barn had been constructed, it had housed over a hundred cattle or more. The stench from the farm was becoming unbearable to the closest neighbours who had tried to speak to certain members of the parish council after they'd got nowhere with the Environmental Health and the Planning Department since Windsor had moved in.

The group of 'concerned neighbours', as they preferred to call themselves, had since learnt that certain parish councillors had labelled them as a 'pressure group', which they found offensive. They felt the council was failing in their duty to listen to the parishioners. The group had met up a few nights ago, when it had been convenient for everyone to attend and put a plan of action in place. It was decided that they would arrive at staggered times and sit separately, dotted throughout the venue.

Natalie and her son, Ben, sat at the rear of the hall. Extra seats were needed as the residents continued to fill the large room. At the front were two members of the parish council, one of whom was also a Hereford County Councillor. The last of the residents entered, and the doors were shut behind them. A hush descended until the chairman of the parish council, Gordon Abbott, stood to address the room.

"Good evening, everyone. For those of you who don't know me, my name is Gordon Abbott, and I've recently been appointed the chairman of the parish council. Before we begin tonight's public meeting concerning the issues raised by certain members of the community, I would like us to hold a two-minute silence for Reverend Paul Gains, who sadly lost his life last night."

"You mean who was murdered last night?" a man from the back shouted.

Abbott nodded. "You're right, he was. A crime that has shocked our community. I'm hoping that anyone who has any knowledge of the crime will come forward to assist the police with their enquiries. I've been assured there will be a police presence in the village over the next forty-eight hours or thereabouts, so please, I'm begging you, if you know anything, come forward and contact the officer in charge of the case. I have her name here somewhere. Where did I put it? Ah, yes, here it is. She's called Detective Inspector Sara Ramsey from West Mercia Police. We need to punish the people who carried out this heinous crime on a much-loved member of our community. Let's begin the silence."

The room fell deadly silent; the only sound was that of people breathing. At the end of the two minutes, Gordon picked up a sheet of paper and read from it. "Before we get this meeting underway, I'd like to read out a note I've been given by Ralph Windsor, regarding the situation at Hazel Farm." He then read out a troubling note that had a threatening tone to it, in which Windsor stated how intimidated he'd felt by the actions of certain residents of the village and the way these people continued to bombard the authorities with unwarranted complaints about his business. He also pointed out that he'd felt harassed and was on the verge of a mental breakdown because of dealing with the added stress.

The crowd murmured throughout the speech. Then, after Gordon finished what he had to say, Alex Parry, the county councillor, stood and read out a letter from Windsor's solicitor, which had an equally threatening tone to it. In it, it stated that anyone who continued to harass Mr Windsor would be pursued through the legal system and taken to court.

Natalie nudged her knee against her son's. "This isn't good. It isn't supposed to be the Ralph Windsor show. It should be about us, the villagers, having the freedom of speech to air our grievances."

Ben leaned over and whispered, "It'll be all right, Mum. Our group will speak up. They won't let the bastard get away with it. You've seen how many have shown up tonight. Let the community have their say about this. He'll be the one who ends up with egg on his face."

Natalie smiled at her son, but deep down, she had a sinking feeling gnawing at her insides.

Once Councillor Parry had finished reading the letter from the solicitor, the meeting was opened up to the audience who had attended. Two closest neighbours stood and spoke in favour of the farmer, stating they smelled nothing offensive coming from the site and that the noise had got better over the past few months because of the adjustments the farmer had made to his business.

Natalie couldn't believe what she was hearing. She could tell by the way her son was fidgeting and breathing heavily beside her he was getting himself worked up into a right state. She patted his hand. "Don't react. Let the people speak."

"He's rallied everyone he knows from this community and where he lived previously to bat on his behalf, Mum. It's not right. He can't be allowed to get away with this, and those twats on the council… bloody hell, they've come out on his side. Unbiased my arse. Look at them. They're as thick as thieves with him."

"It stinks, I know. Looks like the parish council has been taking backhanders, just like we suspected, doesn't it?"

"You're not wrong. I can't wait to meet up with the others and see what they have to say about all of this. I have to tell you, it's sticking in my throat this evening."

One after the other, the farmer's associates stood to speak on his behalf, from the men who worked on his farm to the man who was classed as the farmer's nutritionist. Regrettably, no one raised their voice about the disruption and impact that had affected their lives since the farm had been recategorised. That was until Jason Holland spoke up to address the room.

Jason cleared his throat and said, "I live directly opposite the farm, and yes, I have had to report the farmer to the authorities many times. The impact his business has had on my family's lives has been nothing short of horrific. The road outside our property is always filthy. The manure is transported from the farm by tractor, up to twenty times a day. The kerbstones outside the property have been removed and replaced by tarmac because they were always getting damaged. The entrance isn't wide enough, the swing the lorries have to take to get onto the site is ridiculous, and what is the parish council doing about it? Absolutely bugger all, that's what! How much has he paid you to read out his letters tonight? What's the matter? Is he illiterate, unable to read? Why do you continue to take his side? I appreciate this is a farming community, and we accept that we're expected to put up with a certain level of smell, but this is beyond disgusting. Even visitors travelling through the village have mentioned the odour on the Facebook group page. We're not the only ones complaining about the issue, and yet nothing, absolutely zilch, is being done about it. Why? And as for the people living right in front of the farm saying they can't smell or hear anything, I suggest they visit the Ear, Nose and Throat Department to get checked over."

Well, the room erupted after that. The Ralph Windsor supporters shouted and accused Jason of all sorts, mostly of hate speech and incitement, for having the courage to stand up and be counted.

The rest of their group, who had put a plan in action for this evening, disappointingly remained silent. The chairman did his best to calm everyone down, but his efforts proved to be in vain. In the end, he drew the meeting to a halt and demanded that everyone leave the hall.

Being at the back, Natalie and Ben were some of the first to leave. They walked to the edge of the car park and watched as the residents filed out of the hall, anger still showing on most of their faces.

Ben leaned in and asked, "Well, what did you make of all that, Ma?"

"Not good, son, not good at all. If nothing else, it's told us we can't trust the parish council members. Try to get the others' attention. We'll see if we can have another meeting to discuss what our next move should be after the debacle that has taken place here this evening."

"You stay put. I'll try to round them up as they leave."

Natalie leaned against the lamppost and made out she was scrolling through her phone whilst keeping one eye on the commotion taking place over to her right between Jason and one of the other neighbours who had spoken up in defence of Windsor. Angry words and shoves took place until another couple of residents were forced to intervene.

"Come on, gents, this won't solve anything, falling out like this. Maybe you've forgotten what was said at the start of the meeting. We all bowed our heads and held a moment's silence for Paul Gains. Or has that slipped your minds? Have some respect for his family. I know they're not here tonight but..." another member of the parish council said.

"Maybe the meeting shouldn't have taken place this evening, it's obvious emotions are running high right now," the neighbour said. He offered to shake Jason's hand.

Jason reluctantly accepted the gesture.

"I agree. Paul wouldn't want us falling out about this. But I stand by what I said in there. You're a liar."

Natalie cringed as the argument kicked off again. Ben joined her.

"What the fuck is going on over there?"

"Keep out of it. Let them bicker amongst themselves. Did you have time to speak with the others?"

"I did. They're going to come back to our house without making it obvious."

"Good, let's set off then. Here, give me your hand. My legs are a bit wobbly, not sure if I'll be able to make it to the car or not."

"Get away with you. You've got plenty of fight in you yet, Mum."

Natalie kissed him on the cheek. "If you say so."

Ben opened the passenger door for her and then jumped behind the steering wheel and set off. They didn't have far to travel, only to the end of the village. They owned a beautiful bungalow. The only downside to owning a property at this end of the village was that the farm was immediately behind them. Although they had a patch of woodland between them and the farm, at this time of the year, when the trees had shed all their leaves, they had a bird's-eye view of the barn for which the farmer had made a retrospective planning application. Natalie was old school. She believed cows belonged in fields, grazing in their natural habitat, not stored in barns where there was nothing more than spitting distance between the suffering beasts. Was this what their world had come to? She had carried out some intensive research on this type of business, and apparently, this new venture had come about because of public pressure. Farmers felt obligated to entertain the idea of keeping their livestock inside because people refused to pay a decent price for beef at the supermarket checkouts.

Gone were the days when people had the money to visit their local butcher for a good cut of meat. Nowadays, all people could afford was what the supermarkets offered and, even then, the price was rising at a phenomenal rate.

Natalie rushed through to the kitchen to fill the kettle. "Ben, will you get the cups and saucers out for me?"

"Won't mugs do? It's such a faff getting all the fine china out and putting it all away again, just to impress the bloody neighbours."

Natalie gave him one of her 'how dare you challenge me' looks. "Just do it, son. Don't question everything I ask you to do."

Ben rolled his eyes and held his hands up. "I wasn't. I wouldn't dare."

The doorbell rang.

"Saved by the bell. I'll let our visitors in." Natalie breezed out of the kitchen, relieved that her legs felt back to normal since they'd come home.

Jason and Mandy Holland were the first to arrive. Jason's usual smile was missing when he entered the hallway and brushed past Natalie. Mandy's shoulders were slumped in despair. She slipped off her coat and handed it to Natalie to hang up on the stand.

"Are you all right, love?"

Mandy stared at her. "Are you? It was farcical, that's what it was, bloody ludicrous."

"I agree. We didn't stand a chance once Windsor started dishing out the intimidation and threats via his solicitor."

"You mean via the twats from the parish council? What kind of idiots do they take us for?"

"Yeah, that meeting was the least impartial one I've ever had the misfortune of attending over the years."

"Well, Jason is livid with how it went, and rightly so."

The doorbell rang, cutting off their conversation. "Go through to the kitchen. Ben's in there, sorting out the drinks. I'll let the others in."

Mandy turned on her heel and went through to the kitchen. Natalie put her shoulders back and slotted a smile in place, then opened the door. Standing on the doorstep were Linda Roland plus Jackie and Matt Falcon. She welcomed them and was about to close the door when she spotted Doreen pulling into the driveway. "Go through. Doreen and I will join you in a moment."

"Sorry to keep you waiting, my car was blocked in outside the village hall. First there, last out. The men blocking me in were standing around chatting and refusing to move, ignorant buggers."

"It's fine, you're not late. The others have only just arrived. Give me your coat. Don't worry about taking off your shoes. It's dry out there tonight, unlike last night."

"Wasn't it vile? Poor Paul, I was mortified to hear of his passing when I visited the corner shop this morning. I had to slap down that cow behind the counter, treating the news as gossip and mentioning it to everyone who entered the shop. If we didn't live so far away from the city centre, I would boycott the bloody shop. Some people have no compassion."

"I couldn't agree more. Let's go through to the kitchen to dissect what happened this evening and what we intend to do about it."

They linked arms and joined the rest of the group.

The meeting became heated quickly. Jason vented his anger, not afraid to speak out and tell the others what he thought of them for neglecting their duty to go into battle. "I was the only one who had the balls to stand up and confront the bastard. Where were all of you when it counted?"

Ben was the first to speak up. "That's not fair, Jason. We were right behind you, as always. It was the other residents in the village who backed out of voicing their opinions because of the threats Windsor had issued at the start of the meeting."

Jason jabbed a thumb at his chest. "And I was the only one to have the courage to counter that intimidation and speak up for our rights. We sat here a few nights ago, thrashed out what everyone's roles were going to be, and you guys clammed up. Some support you turned out to be."

The rest of the group bowed their heads in shame.

Eventually, Doreen spoke up. "In our defence, when we had our meeting the other night, Paul Gains was still alive. I believe his death overshadowed our plans, put us, and perhaps other members of this community, on the back foot from the outset."

"Maybe that was the parish council's plan," Ben said. "No one could have predicted his death playing a major part in tonight's proceedings."

"I know, you're right, Ben. I don't think anyone realised the impact Paul's death would have on us all," Linda said. "Personally, it choked me up throughout the evening. I had a lump the size of a melon sitting in my throat that I had trouble shifting."

Natalie reached out a hand to her. "I was the same, love. It takes a lot for me to get worked up about someone not related to me dying, but he was so different, such an integral part of the village. I'm sure we are all going to miss him." She raised her cup and encouraged the others to do the same. "To Paul. RIP, dear man."

After a moment's pause, Mandy said, "Maybe he would have come out on our side tonight if someone hadn't killed him. About that, I heard on the grapevine that he had his stomach sliced open first before the killer hung him. Who would do such a thing, and to a vicar, of all people?"

The room fell silent, leaving everyone to process what Linda had said.

Natalie left her seat and walked across the room to the pantry. She removed a chocolate cake from the middle shelf and returned to the kitchen. "I don't know about you, but there's only one way I can overcome a bout of depression, and that's by munching on a piece of chocolate cake. Anyone else up for it?"

Ben stared at his mother and shook his head in disbelief. "Mum doesn't need an excuse to get the cakes out. I'll have mine later, if there's any left."

Jason and Matt also declined the offer, but the ladies in the group lapped up the prospect of having a sugar rush to combat their bout of the blues.

"Does anyone want a can of beer rather than tea?" Ben asked the men sitting around the table.

"I'm fine with tea, and I'm driving. The last thing I need right now is to get caught and have my licence taken away from me," Jason said, who was a travelling salesman for a blinds company.

But Matt took Ben up on his offer, and he left the table again.

"So, the leading question is, where do we go from here?" Linda plucked up the courage to ask moments later.

Jason crossed his arms, his expression soured by the events that had already taken place. "I'm out of suggestions. What's the point in us holding these discussions any more if people aren't prepared to step up to the plate when the opening arises? We're the ones who begged the parish council to hold the public meeting in the first place, only to fail at the first hurdle, so what's the use in us debating what we should do next?"

"Don't be like that, Jason," Doreen said. "Tonight, or should I say today, what with the sad news about Paul circulating the village all day, well, it's exceptional circumstances that none of us could have perceived taking place to railroad our plan. The least we can do is discuss where we should go from here."

Jason stood and tucked his chair under the table. "I sense there's always going to be an excuse as to why certain people around this table ditch a plan once it has been put in place. Come on, Mandy, let's go."

Mandy's gaze drifted around the table, and her cheeks reddened. "But I want to stay, darling. I'd feel I was letting the side down if I left now."

"Ha, shame you didn't feel that way at the village hall tonight. You can catch a lift with someone else or walk home then. I'm out of here, and don't count on me showing up at any meetings in the future, either. And yes, take me off the WhatsApp group while you're at it. That's been annoying the hell out of me since I joined it. There's a reason I don't entertain those kinds of apps on my phone. They are an intrusion, going off every five minutes or so. Give me a break." He stormed out of the kitchen, and seconds later, the front door slammed.

Mandy stared out of the kitchen window, shaking her head. "I'm sorry, he shouldn't have said that. He didn't speak for both of us, I can assure you. I'm determined to give this group the support it needs to continue."

"That's great, Mandy. Perhaps Jason will have second thoughts once he's calmed down a little," Natalie said.

"Nope, I doubt it. Once he's got a bee in his bonnet about something, that's it, there's no going back for him... ever, I'm afraid. Stubborn as a mule, that one, just like his father."

"Never mind, I'm sure we'll cope without him."

However, Jason had always been the one with the brightest ideas for the group to chew over during their discussions. Someone who the rest of them looked up to for advice. Without him to steer the ship, where was that going to leave them? Natalie suspected the evening was going to flop, and she was proved right half an hour later. The ideas being bounced around were what she considered futile compared to what Jason had presented to them when their campaign had started.

The group left with the promise they would all consider which direction they should go in next.

THE FOLLOWING DAY, the killers were parked outside a house in Wilton, close to the village hall.

"That's her car, I'm sure it is. I remember she had all the stickers put on last year, and she told me that once the job was done, how much she hated it."

"That's typical when we do something on a whim. At least it's getting dark now. As soon as she leaves the house, I'll get out of the car and approach her."

"I was about to suggest the same. Hold on, the front door is opening. Go on, get out now, so it's not so obvious." He watched as his associate walked across the road and spoke with Victoria Holt, otherwise known as the secretary for the parish council, who was also the mobile hairdresser for the community.

She smiled at his associate and removed her appointment book from her bag.

His associate returned to the car.

"Well? How did you get on?"

"She's going to drop by the house later, at seven, but I know where she's off to now, so we can make our move before then."

"Excellent news. We're getting good at this sneaky behaviour; it can only bode well for us in the future. Let's face it, we've got a few locals we need to get rid of."

Victoria drove off, and they followed her to her next location.

"We'll give it five minutes, let her get settled inside the house, just in case she forgets to take any of her equipment in with her and has to return to the car."

"I feel bad about this."

"Why? She's part of the group we have targeted. Don't go getting cold feet on me now."

"I'm not. I just said I feel bad about it, but then I felt cruel about killing the vicar."

He laughed. "It'll pass. You also said that you got a buzz from seeing him take his last breath."

"I know. I'll keep my mouth shut."

"I should." He laughed again, and his accomplice sank deeper into their seat. "Don't get too comfortable. She told you this would be a quick visit; therefore, we need to stay alert."

"You can. Wake me up when she reappears."

"Not likely. Stay awake, you'll feel better about it."

FIFTEEN MINUTES LATER, Victoria came out of the house. She loaded up the car again and set off.

"We'll make our move up the road, where it widens. I'll whizz past her."

He followed the pink-stickered car for a couple of miles and then made his move and drove past it. The road narrowed soon after, and he let out a relieved sigh. "That was close. I didn't think I was going to make it. You'd better put your mask on." He removed his from the pocket in the door and slipped it on, holding the steering wheel with his knees while he carried out the manoeuvre.

He checked his rear-view mirror and saw Victoria singing along to the music and tapping her fingers as she was driving. All seemed to be well in her little bubble.

"Are you ready for this? I'm going to brake and block the road. You need to be prepared to get out and sprint back to the car. We need to get her car door open before she realises what's going on and locks us out."

"I'm ready, but what if it goes wrong?"

"It won't. Stop being so negative. We got away with killing the vicar the other night, didn't we?"

"Yes, but this is different."

"How? It doesn't matter. We don't have time for this discussion." He hit the brakes and shoved his associate out of the car, then threw his door open and scrambled out, sensing his accomplice was going to cock things up.

Victoria's eyes widened, and she screamed. Her instincts took over, and he heard the clunk as the car doors locked.

"Shit, I've got a crowbar in the boot." He ran back to the car and collected the tool that he was about to use as a weapon on the woman for pissing him off after he smashed through the glass.

At first the crowbar bounced off the driver's window until he remembered his mate telling him the weakest point to any pane of glass was the corner. He changed his technique, and eventually, it gave way.

Victoria screamed. "What are you doing? Get away from me." She reached for her mobile on the passenger seat.

He seized it and threw it on the ground, then smashed it with his heel. "Don't try anything else. Get out of the car."

"No, I won't. You can't make me."

He inserted his arm through the broken window. Victoria tried to bat his fingers away from the button before he could open the door. With his free hand, he reached over and grasped both of her wrists. She wriggled, but his grip held firm and he was able to get the door open.

His accomplice stood back until Victoria was out of the car.

"Get the tape and put it over her mouth."

Victoria screamed with all her might, recognising this would be her last opportunity to alert someone of the danger she was in,

He thumped her in the mouth. "Christ, stupid bitch, you did some damage to my inner ear. You're going to pay for that."

"Fuck off. If you think I'm going to take this lying down, you've got another think coming."

Victoria kicked out, her trainers connecting with his shin.

"Feisty cow, ain't ya? I wouldn't bother trying to fight your way out of this one. We've got everything covered. Your life is going to end tonight."

"I don't think so." Victoria jabbed her elbows in his stomach and took off down the road they'd travelled on.

Still winded, he took up the chase and gained on her

quickly. He passed a gate to the field on the right, and a new plan formed in his mind. He jumped on her back, and she toppled to the ground beneath his weight, but even then, she didn't give up the fight. She squirmed and wriggled free, but he pounced again before she could get to her feet.

"Give it up. I won't let you get away from me again."

She spat at him. "Never, not while there's still a breath in my body. I've had worse fuckers than you to deal with over the years."

"I doubt it," he countered and yanked her onto her feet once more. He pushed her towards the gate and opened it.

"What are you doing?" his accomplice asked, still holding the piece of tape in their hands.

"Change of plan. Because of her attempt to flee, we're going to teach her a lesson here."

"You don't scare me, you're amateurs, I can tell," Victoria goaded them.

"We'll show you what type of amateurs we are, bearing in mind we've already done away with the vicar." He laughed at the shock registering on her face. "That's right. Still think we're amateurs, do you?"

"Please, let me go. I don't deserve to be treated this way."

"Yeah, that's probably what the vicar thought as well; it didn't save him either."

"But why? Why did you kill Paul?"

He jabbed her in the back to make her move, tired of listening to her whining voice. "You don't need to know the ins and outs."

"What are we going to do with her?" asked his accomplice.

"Get the rope out of the car and the duffle bag. I'm going to make sure we punish her for trying to escape."

Victoria dug her heels into the grass as soon as they entered the gate. "I refuse to go any further."

He slammed a fist into her stomach and then clouted her in the jaw. She sank to the ground, out cold. He snatched the tape from his partner and put it over her mouth, then dragged her out of view, in case any other cars passed by. His accomplice arrived with the equipment.

"I'm going to shift the cars. I'll be right back. Clout her with this if she wakes up." He handed his partner the crowbar.

"Don't be long. She's not going to be easy to handle."

"You'll be fine. Just bash her over the head with the bar." He ran off to see to the vehicles and returned once he'd straightened them and parked them behind each other. "Did she wake up?"

"No, not at all. What's next?"

He opened the bag and withdrew a hammer.

"Oh my, what are you going to do with that, or shouldn't I ask?"

He laughed and tapped the hammer on his palm. "You'll find out soon enough. Let's drag her to the side, away from the gate where someone is likely to see us." With the hedge now shielding them, he hit the hammer against her shin. The sound of the bone shattering made him grin.

Victoria woke up and tried to scream, but the tape kept her quiet.

"Ah, it's so good not hearing your whining voice or your piercing scream in my ear. Hurt, did it?"

Victoria nodded, slowly. Her gaze flitting between the two people towering over her.

"Right, now you're going to accept your punishment, because it's what the people in our community are crying out for, to see you and the other parish councillors suffer, the way you're making us suffer."

Victoria frowned and shook her head. She tried to speak, but it came out as an inaudible mumble.

"You know damn well what I'm talking about. Don't tell me otherwise."

Victoria's head swept from side to side.

"Maybe we should give her a break. She looks petrified."

"As anyone would in her situation. Get over it. We've come too far to back out now. I'm guessing that she has recognised our voices. If we let her go, she'll run straight to the police."

"Mmm... mmmm." Victoria tried her best to communicate with them.

The hammer came down on her other leg. Tears welled up and dripped onto her cheeks.

"Now her arms," he said, a buzz trickling down his spine as he raised the hammer and delivered a substantial blow that came down heavily on Victoria's lower arm, again shattering her bone. He got off on the fear dwelling in her eyes.

"That's enough. I get the feeling you're getting a thrill from this. Get it over with before someone comes along and catches us in the act."

"Us? I'm the one doing all the work, as usual."

His partner turned and walked out of the gate. "I'll wait in the car."

"Whatever. I'll be with you in a while."

He took the knife from the duffle bag beside him and ran a finger down the blade, and then placed the tip on Victoria's right cheek. She flinched and turned her head away from him. He laughed, and using the tip of the blade, forced her to face him again.

"Don't worry, I won't draw this out, if that's what you want?"

After a few seconds' pause, Victoria nodded, the fear still clear in her green eyes. He plunged the knife into her stomach; she let out a cry that the tape muffled, and her eyes flickered shut and then sprang open again.

"I thought that would be enough to kill you. Maybe I was wrong. Let's see if this will hit the spot." A sinister chuckle erupted, and he slashed the knife across her throat.

Her gaze held his for the briefest of moments before her eyes closed for the last time. He watched her chest rise and fall until her breathing stopped. Then he wiped the blood off the knife in the long grass beside her, collected his duffle bag and returned to the car.

CHAPTER 4

"Another day and yet another crime scene for us to attend," Sara grumbled the following morning. She hadn't been at work long before the call came in from Lorraine, requesting her attendance at a farmer's field out near Wilton. The frostiness coming from Carla had melted. However, Sara still hadn't got a clue as to what had set her partner off, regarding the vicar and the case.

"Two murders within a few days of each other and in the same village. What are the odds of that?" Carla replied.

"Yeah, exactly. I have a feeling, gnawing at my insides. We could be looking at the same killers carrying out the deed."

"What? Without us even seeing the second victim, how can you say that?"

Sara faced her for a moment and then returned her gaze to the road ahead. "Are you serious? For a start, how often are we called out to Wilton? No, I'll answer that question for you… never. And you don't think it's suspicious being called out twice to the same location within a couple of days of the vicar being killed?"

"Christ, I've just had a horrifying thought. What if we show up and discover the victim is his wife?"

"Don't even go there. We've had a patrol car on call monitoring the village since his death. I think it's unlikely. Bugger, at least I'm hoping you're wrong."

"What do we know about the victim?"

"Nothing yet, other than she was found in a field with multiple wounds."

"Shocking. Why in a field? Was she dumped there? Did she meet someone at the location?"

Sara laughed. "One thing at a time, partner. Let's get to the scene and observe what's happened for ourselves first, and then try to figure out the logistics of the crime."

"Oops, sorry. I'm guilty of jumping ahead of myself. I suppose that's the frustration talking because we haven't really got very far with the first crime yet, and now we have a second one thrust upon us."

"True. As a team, we're doing our best, and while it's only been a couple of days since Paul Gains was killed, there were many people on the list who we need to chase up and speak to. And now, we have another crime on our hands—sorry, I should have said murder to deal with—and we're back to square one. We're not far from the location now."

"Let's hope Lorraine finds some clues for us to follow. We're in dire need of something to help us solve this investigation, especially if we suspect the crimes are linked. I bet when the word gets out that there has been another murder, the villagers will be crapping themselves."

"Let's put it this way, with the residents on full alert, it's only going to make it more difficult for the murderers to choose another victim, if we are looking at a serial killer scenario here."

"I suppose that's true. They must have some guts, though, to go after the vicar in the first place."

Sara ran a hand around her chin. "We're in agreement there." She wound her way through the lanes outside the village until she drew up behind the SOCO vans. The road had been cordoned off just behind the vans. "This is ridiculous. What's the point in having the cordon here? It's not like there are very many places for cars to turn around here. Will you get that sorted while I have a chat with Lorraine?"

"On it now. Shall I tell them to block the road at both ends?"

"Yep."

They exited the car, and Sara went in search of her pathologist friend.

"Are you here, Lorraine?"

"Behind the hedge. Don't come near if you haven't got the correct attire on, though."

"I'll be two seconds." She flew back to the car and removed two suits from the boot. Carla joined her. "I'm guessing you received some stick from the uniformed officers, judging by the look on your face."

"I gave as good as I got. I had to pull rank on one of them, the cheeky shit."

"Ignore them. Don't let them spoil your day. I'll have a word with Jeff when we get back to base, make him aware of the situation."

"I wouldn't bother. It's not worth all the hassle. It's sorted now."

"Okay. Let's get our suits on and see what Lorraine has for us."

A few minutes later, they made their way through the gate and into the field. "We'd better go the whole hog and slip our booties over our shoes."

They supported each other and slipped their protective covers on before they joined Lorraine, who was about ten feet away from them.

"Ah, you're here, at last. What kept you?"

"We came as soon as we could. What have we got here?"

"Female victim this time. Multiple broken bones to both her legs and arm. A knife wound to the stomach and her throat is cut."

"The killer wanted to make sure there was no chance of her surviving, is that it?" Sara asked.

"You tell me."

"All right, there's no need to snap my head off. It was a genuine question or appraisal of the situation."

"I apologise. I'm not having the best of days." Lorraine stared off over the fields.

"How come? Or are you going to leave us dangling?"

"Someone knocked me off my bike this morning and caused thousands of pounds' worth of damage to my baby."

"Ouch, sorry to hear that. Did they stop?"

"Oh yes. The fucker tried to tell me the accident wasn't his fault."

"And was it?" Sara cringed.

"How dare you? I was following the rules of the road. There was a lorry in front of me and this twat was behind me. He overtook me and had to pull in quickly because there was a car coming in the opposite direction."

"And he knocked you off your bike?"

"Yes, swore blind that he didn't see me. I told him exactly what I thought of him and rang the police. He said he wasn't taking the blame for the accident and buggered off."

"Did you get his registration number?"

Lorraine narrowed her eyes. "What do you take me for? Of course I frigging did."

"Problem solved. We'll arrest him for leaving the scene of an accident. Bingo bongo."

"And who's going to pay for the damage to my bike?"

"His insurance... unless he isn't insured."

Lorraine winked and tapped a finger on her nose. "Now you're understanding the situation better."

"Sorry if you thought I was slow on the uptake. Leave it with me. I'll track the bugger down and get the money out of him for you."

"Thanks, Sara, you're a genuine friend."

"Don't mention it. What kind of damage was there to your bike? Actually, sod the bike. How are you?"

"I've got a few grazes here and there. My suit is well padded, but I reckon my bike is going to cost thousands to repair, plus I'll have the inconvenience of having it off the road for weeks."

"Can you use the van while the bike's in the garage?"

"I'm going to have to. The neighbours will love that. They send a posse around every time I take it home with me."

"What is wrong with people? Can you park it around the corner?"

"It doesn't matter. I'll get it sorted, one way or another. Enough doom and gloom and general chit-chatting. We've got a crime scene to attend to."

They moved closer to the body.

Sara cast her gaze over the wounds the woman had suffered. "Do you think she was tortured, or were the wounds carried out in a fit of rage after she died?"

"I won't be able to answer that until I've performed the PM."

"Next question, bear with me on this one..."

Lorraine turned her way.

"Could the crimes be connected?"

Lorraine frowned. "Just because of the location?"

"Yes, I suppose. Carla and I were discussing it in the car on the way over here. We've never really been out this way before, and now we've had two murders within a few days."

"If you put it like that, then maybe there's a connection.

The MOs couldn't be more different, though, not that it means anything. Some serial killers prefer to switch their MOs now and again anyway, you know, to keep the police on their toes."

"Did she have any ID on her?"

"No. You probably didn't see it when you arrived, but her car was parked in the lane. It might be worth you having a look at that before we get it towed to the lab for examination."

"Brilliant. I wasn't aware, your vans were blocking our view. So, what are we saying here, that she drove to the location?"

"Either that or someone used her car to bring her here."

Continuing to stare at the body, Sara asked, "Was her body dumped or was she killed here?"

"That's where you come in, regarding the car. By the amount of blood at the scene, I'm inclined to believe she was killed here."

"Anything else you can give us at this stage?"

"Nothing much, sorry. We're not going to hang around out here for long, not with the number of grey clouds in the area."

"I don't blame you. We'll give the car the once-over then."

"Make sure you cover your heads and put gloves on."

"That goes without saying."

Sara and Carla left the field and crossed the road to where the car was parked.

"A very distinctive car it should be easy to find the owner if we draw a blank inside." Sara opened the boot first and rummaged through the bag in there. "Ah, I don't have to be Einstein to know that she's a hairdresser."

"Does she have any business cards in there?"

Sara searched the pockets on the front of the bag. "Good thinking. Victoria Holt. Can you get the ball rolling on that for me? I'll keep checking to see if I can find her address in the glove box." She handed Carla the card, which only had the woman's name and telephone number typed on it.

Carla took a few steps back and rang the station.

Sara opened the passenger door and leaned in to check the glove box. She found a small wallet. Inside was the woman's driving licence, confirming her address. She took a photo of it and placed it back in the glove box.

Carla ended her call. "The team is getting onto it now. How did you get on?"

"I found her address. I'll tell Lorraine, and then we'll shoot over there, see if anyone has been missing her, or not."

A tech was photographing the victim, and Lorraine was discussing with another member of her team about transferring the body to the mortuary.

Sara and Carla stood back until they had finished their conversation.

"Sorry to keep you, ladies. Did you find anything?"

"She's a hairdresser, Victoria Holt. We've got her address; we're going over there now. I wanted to check in with you first before we left."

"Thanks for that. I'll make a note of her name up here." Lorraine prodded her temple with a finger. "Ouch, I wish I hadn't done that."

"Let me have a look at you." Sara took a step towards her, but Lorraine retreated.

"I'm fine. Stop your fussing now."

Sara's eyes narrowed, and she stomped her foot on the grass. "You can be so bloody stubborn, infuriating even, at times."

"I know I can. And you worry too much. Be told, woman, I'll be okay. Now, if you'll excuse me, I should get back to work."

"I know, I know, the clouds are against you. Promise me

you'll make an appointment with your doctor ASAP, or better still, take a trip to A and E."

"I'll do no such thing. Now do one. Get out of my hair before I lose my rag with you."

Sara pulled a face at her good friend. "Pardon me for caring about what happens to you."

"I know you mean well, but do you really think I would have reported for duty if I didn't feel up to it? Credit me with a modicum of sense, Sara. Also, you have enough on your plate at the moment, what with the funeral to think about. So stop stressing about me."

"That's me told then. Okay. You know where I am if you need me, day or night, right?"

"Yes, boss. Now get out of my hair and let me get on."

Sara smiled and turned back to the car. She and Carla removed their protective suits and put them in the black sack that had been tied to the gate.

THE LARGE, detached house was at the opposite end of the village to the vicarage.

"Seems a tad fancy for a hairdresser to own," Carla said.

They left the car.

"We shouldn't make assumptions; she might have a wealthy husband, or she could have inherited this place when either of their parents passed away."

"That's true."

The front garden had a neatly manicured lawn. There was an arch leading around to the side, covered in roses, that had dropped their leaves and flowers, although there were a few unopened buds at the top that had gone brown in the rain.

Sara rang the bell, but there was no answer. She walked across the lawn, through the arch, to the back garden, which was a delight, even at this time of the year. The back door was locked, and there was no sign of life.

"Hello, who are you? And what are you doing in my friend's garden?" a woman's voice called over the fence.

Sara crossed the lawn to speak with the woman. She showed her ID as proof. "Sorry, we were hoping to find someone home. Can you tell me who lives here?"

The older woman frowned. "Are you having a laugh? You just told me you were from the police, and here you are, asking me who owns the house. I'm not falling for that one. Now tell me the truth. What are you doing here?"

"Sorry, you're right to question me. We know that Victoria Holt lives here. I wondered who she lives with. Does she have a husband?"

"This is her parents' house. She moved back in with them a few years back when she split up with that useless thug of a boyfriend of hers. He beat her black and blue, he did. It was shocking to see the state of her. If anyone had done that to me in my younger days, I would have knifed the bastard."

"I know I shouldn't say this, but I agree with you. Are her parents at home?"

"No, you're out of luck. They're travelling around the UK for the next two months, making the most of the weather before the winter sets in. I don't blame them either."

"I don't suppose you have a number for them, do you?"

"I've got it inside. Is something wrong?"

"I simply need to chat with them. Travelling in what, by the way?"

"They bought one of those fancy campervans. It cost them a fortune, it did, luxurious inside. If I had my time over at their age, I would have done exactly the same thing. Sod going abroad, not when there are so many beautiful areas to visit in this country."

"Sounds like a wonderful holiday to me. Do you know where they are at the moment?"

"They only set off a couple of weeks ago. Their plan was to start off in Cornwall and drive up to John O'Groats, but nothing was set in stone. They were going to see how the mood took them. Let me get the number for you."

Sara turned to take in the length of the garden. "I bet this place will be a wilderness by the time they get back, now that Victoria is gone."

"Gone? What do you mean?" The woman had returned without Sara realising it.

"Sorry, umm… we have some bad news. Victoria's body was found earlier today."

"Oh my, I need to sit down. My legs have gone all wobbly."

"Are you all right? We'll come round."

"There's a gate at the side of the house. I might need to take one of my tablets."

"We'll be there in a jiffy."

Sara and Carla retraced their steps and then sprinted out of the gate and into the garden next door.

"I hope we're not too late," Sara said.

"Should I call for an ambulance, just in case?"

"Leave it for now. She might be able to pop a miracle pill that will put her on her feet again."

"Maybe we should all have one of those lying around."

Sara grinned and rushed over to the woman. "Hi there. How are you feeling?"

"Like death warmed up. I need one of my heart tablets, they're in the kitchen. Open the dresser drawer. There's a pot of pills in there."

"Carla, will you try to find them?"

Sara knelt beside the woman who had made it to the

patio set outside an extension of her home. "Don't fret, we're here with you."

The woman clutched a hand to her chest. "Please tell your friend to hurry."

Sara left the woman and darted into the kitchen. Carla was searching every drawer in there but the right one.

"Get a grip. She said they were in the dresser, over there, under the stairs."

"Shit, I didn't see it tucked away back there."

Sara ran over and yanked the drawer out. Off to the side was a small pot. "I've found them. Get me a glass or a mug of water, whichever is easiest."

They met up by the back door.

Sara glanced out to see the woman collapsed in the chair. "Fuck!" She read the label. It said to place a tablet under the tongue. She popped the lid and removed one of the small blue pills, which she put under the woman's tongue. "Here, take a sip of water."

The woman refused the water.

"Don't force her, Sara. The tablet will probably need to dissolve in her mouth."

"Gosh, you're right. How stupid of me. Hello, can you tell me your name?"

"It's Amy Yates."

"Do you need us to call anyone for you, Amy? A friend or a member of your family, perhaps?"

"No, the pill won't take that long until it starts to work. I'm feeling better already, dear. I'm sorry I've caused you so much trouble."

Sara rose to her feet and offered Amy the glass of water. "Are you allowed to have a drink yet?"

"I'd like to leave it a few more minutes, just to be on the safe side."

"Please, let me call someone for you," Sara pleaded.

"Oh, all right, maybe you'd better. I was feeling off colour last week, and the doctor said I should look after myself for a week or two."

"Okay, who shall I call?"

"There's no need. My neighbour on the right, Fran, she'll come and sit with me for a little while, until I'm back on my feet again."

Carla nodded. "I'll go."

Sara sat in the chair next to Amy. "I'm sorry if we caused you some distress. May I ask what's wrong with you?"

"It's angina. I've been suffering with it for the past five years. I keep it under control most of the time, but now and again something like this happens, and it knocks me for six."

"I understand. Again, I'm sorry to have been the cause of the problem."

"Hush now, it wasn't your fault. Too nosey for my own good sometimes, I am. I overheard you talking. Is it true?"

Reluctantly, Sara admitted, "Yes, I'm afraid so. I really don't want to add to your stress by talking about it further." She glanced down at the brown address book Amy had in her lap. "Is the number in there for Victoria's mother and father?"

"That's right. I can sort it for you, if you give me a chance to find it."

Carla arrived with the neighbour.

"Oh my dear, Amy. What are we going to do with you?"

"It's not my fault. Well, perhaps it is. The police officers were talking, and I overheard the dreadful news, and the next second my legs gave way beneath me."

Fran sat on the other side of her friend. "What news? Are John and Sandra all right?"

"They are, as far as I know. It's their daughter. Oh, Fran, her body has been found."

"What are you saying? That she's dead?" Fran asked, the colour draining from her cheeks.

"Yes, I don't know how. Perhaps the officers can fill us in. Can you?" Amy asked.

"I think I should contact her parents first, don't you?"

"Of course you must. No, don't go listening to me. Let me find their number for you."

Amy located the page and then passed the book to Sara. She stood and walked away from the ladies to make the call.

"Hello, is that Sandra Holt?"

"It is, and no, I'm not buying anything. I never deal with salespeople over the phone."

"I quite understand. I don't blame you. I'm Detective Inspector Sara Ramsey. I'm so sorry to disturb you on your holiday."

"Oh, what's the matter? It's not our daughter, is it?"

"I'm sorry, yes. I don't really enjoy delivering this sort of news over the phone…"

"What news? What are you trying to tell me, that my daughter has had an accident?"

Sara could hear the woman's husband in the background, demanding to know what was going on.

"I'm putting the phone on speaker because my husband is very concerned now."

"Perhaps it's for the best. I'm sorry to have to inform you that your daughter's body was found this morning."

The couple fell silent until sobbing could be heard.

"What do you mean?" Mr Holt insisted gruffly. "It's all right, Sandra, stop that now. How am I supposed to hear what the inspector has to say?"

"As I've said already, Mr Holt, I really don't like delivering this kind of news over the phone to a victim's next of kin."

"Victim? Why are you calling Victoria that? Tell me what's happened. I have a right to know, now!"

Sara closed her eyes and swallowed. "I'd rather go over the details with you in person. Can you come back home, if it's not too inconvenient for you?"

"What are you talking about? Of course we will. It's going to take us around three hours or more to get there."

"I'll expect to see you at Hereford Police Station around lunchtime."

The phone went dead.

Sara felt bereft.

Carla came and stood beside her and placed a hand on her back. "I don't have to ask how it went. Are you all right?"

"I've had better days."

"Are they coming home?"

"Yes, I've told them I'll meet them at the station in about three hours. God, I hate this job at times."

"I'd hug you if Amy and Fran weren't watching us. I'm sorry, Sara."

"Don't be. I'm not the one who has lost a child. Come on, let's make sure Amy is well enough to be left before we return to base."

VICTORIA'S PARENTS arrived about three and a half hours later. Sara hadn't realised what the time was and was shocked to learn of their arrival when Jeff rang to inform her.

"God, where does the time go around here some days? Do you want to come with me, Carla?"

Her partner took another sip from the coffee one of the team had made only minutes earlier and picked up her notebook. "I'm ready when you are."

They left the office and walked down the stairs to the reception area, where they found the distraught couple waiting for them.

"Can you get Mr and Mrs Holt a drink, Sergeant?"

"It's all in hand, Inspector. Room Two is available for you."

"Thanks." Sara shook the couple's hands and introduced herself and Carla. "If you'd like to follow me, we can discuss the matter in private."

The shell-shocked Mr Holt helped his wife to her feet, and the couple followed Sara and Carla down the hallway. Once they were seated, he demanded, "We want to know everything you know about our daughter's death. Don't hold back, Inspector."

"I'm afraid there's not very much to tell you, not yet. A post-mortem is due to be carried out on your daughter this afternoon. We're hoping that will shed some light on the injuries she's received."

"Which were? Be honest with us, I'm begging you. Don't keep us in the dark. I've heard the police like to do that to families."

"I'm not the type of officer to keep relevant details from the next of kin, sir, I can assure you. So, if I sound vague, it's only because I'm waiting on the report from the pathologist."

"We understand that, Inspector." Mrs Holt wiped a tear away and said, "All we ask is that you keep nothing from us."

"I won't, I promise. I received the call from the pathologist first thing this morning. My partner and I drove out to the scene, which was on the outskirts of Wilton, where your daughter's body was found."

"Where?" Mr Holt asked. He shuffled his chair closer to his wife's and placed an arm around her shoulder.

"In a farmer's field. Before you ask, we don't know how she got there. Her car was found on the road beside the field."

"So, it wasn't an accident. Someone definitely did this to her?" Mrs Holt asked quietly. She clutched her husband's other hand.

"The likelihood is that your daughter was being followed. The pathologist believes she was killed at the scene, not transferred there after her death." She held back, giving them all the information Lorraine had told her, despite them wanting to know everything.

"What injuries did she have? How was she killed?" Mr Holt pressed.

After a moment's hesitation, Sara replied. "She suffered several broken limbs and was stabbed a few times." She intentionally left out the part about the victim's throat being sliced open.

"Oh no, not my baby," Mrs Holt said, fresh tears streaming down her cheeks. "Who would do such a thing?"

"That's what we intend to find out. Perhaps you can fill us in on some details about your daughter's past? When we spoke to your neighbour, Amy, she mentioned that Victoria had moved back home after living with an abusive partner."

"Yes, yes, it has to be that bastard," Mr Holt said, clearly agitated. "The day Victoria told us she was moving back home, she warned me not to get involved, but the minute I saw her, I knew I had to. She had two black eyes and a couple of bruised fingers where he'd pulled them back during an argument. I picked my moment, and once she was settled back with us at home, I went round to have a quiet word with him."

Sara cringed. "And how did that work out?"

He raised an eyebrow. "As you'd expect. The tosser… sorry, excuse my language, ladies, the idiot brings out the worst in me. We had a showdown. He mouthed off, but when I threatened to punch his lights out for him, he ran away, scared. Threatened to call the police. Typical bully when confronted with violence."

"And how did the conversation, I use the term lightly, end?"

"He asked me to leave. Reluctantly, I left the house, but I kept a close eye on my daughter to ensure she didn't contact him again."

"And Victoria was okay with that?"

"Absolutely. Within a few months, our old daughter was back. She'd changed drastically in the time she was with him. We couldn't figure out why that was until I caught him talking to her disrespectfully in our garden one day; he thought they were alone. He turned around and saw me. They both left not long after that, too embarrassed, probably."

"Have you seen him since?"

"Fleetingly, at the supermarket. He was leaving as we were doing our weekly shop. We shared glares, shall we say?"

"And what about Victoria? Has she mentioned recently if she'd seen him?"

"Nothing to me. What about you, Sandra?"

"No, she hasn't uttered his name since she moved back in, nor anyone else's before you ask. That was going to be your next question, wasn't it?"

"You're right, it was. What about asking you if anything had been bothering her? Perhaps someone making advances towards her or even threatening her."

"No, nothing that I can think of. She was a mobile hair-dresser, a very successful one, so it's not like work colleagues have pestered her."

"Did she have any other interests? A hobby, perhaps? Go to the gym to work out? Was she enrolled in an evening class at college? Did she meet up with her friends in the evening and go into town?"

The couple glanced at each other and shook their heads.

"No, nothing that we can think of," Mr Holt replied.

His wife's eyes narrowed as if something had come to mind.

"Have you thought about something, Mrs Holt?"

"I have. Our daughter was the secretary of the parish council. That took up quite a lot of her spare time. I simply didn't associate it with a hobby, if you like, or doing something pleasurable in her spare time."

"I see, thank you, that's interesting."

Mr Holt inclined his head and frowned. "You say that as though it should mean something. May we ask what?"

"I know you've been on your travels, so you probably haven't heard about another murder that has happened in the village in your absence."

"Who?" Mr Holt asked. He hugged his wife tighter.

Sara hesitated for a moment and then said, "The local vicar."

"Paul Gains? Victoria really liked him; she told us he was the salt of the earth. Well, he would be, wouldn't he? Being a vicar, although saying that, even Paul told us that some of his associates were a bit dodgy. I don't mean corrupt, just not all they should be."

Sara frowned. "I don't understand."

"He told Victoria that he often wanted to pull his hair out when speaking to other members of the church because of the way they spoke to people in their flocks. Whereas Paul was very down to earth, listened to people's problems without judging them. Victoria said he was the best vicar they'd had in the village, and that's why he was asked to be on the parish council."

"Interesting to know. Thank you for that."

"I can't believe they're dead, our Victoria and the vicar. Hang on, you're not saying that the same person has done this, are you?"

"At this time, no, there's no way of us knowing if that's the case or not, not until some evidence comes our way."

"But Wilton is a quiet village, not like something off the

TV, like that Midsomer place, where they have murder after murder every damn week. I can't remember the last time we had a death in the village, by natural causes even. Can you, Sandra?"

"There was old Mrs Trott, but she passed away in a nursing home in the end."

"Yes, that's right."

"Thank you for being so open with us. I'm going to give you my card, in case you think of anything else when you leave here."

The couple continued to comfort each other. Now that the conversation had stopped, the emotion had reappeared and was etched deep into their features.

"Is there anything you'd like to ask?"

After a moment's pause, Mr Holt asked, "Would it be possible for us to see her?"

"Absolutely, although not right away. The post-mortem will have to be performed first. I can give your details to the pathologist, and she can call you afterwards and inform you when it would be okay to visit."

Mrs Holt sobbed again, and her husband squeezed her around the shoulders. She turned to face him, and they shared an intimate hug.

"We're never going to see her again. I can't believe it. I think it's only just struck me."

"It's all right, love. We'll get through this together."

Sara tried to swallow down the lump that had appeared in her throat. Once the couple had separated, she asked, "One last thing… can you tell us Justin's address?"

"I think I still have it on my phone." Mrs Holt withdrew her mobile from her handbag and scrolled through her contacts list. "No idea why I've still got it in here. I should have deleted it long ago. Here it is, it's number ten Lester

Road, Eign Hill. The property is in two flats, he rents the upper one. If he's still there, of course."

"We'll check. Thank you, that's a great help. Why don't you go home now and get some rest?"

Mr Holt nodded and pushed back his chair. "Yes, I think we'll do that. There's nothing else you can think of to ask the inspector, love, is there?"

He helped his wife to her feet. "I can't think of anything." She tottered unsteadily. "Damn legs, they're all wobbly."

"You're welcome to sit here for a while, if you'd rather," Sara offered.

"No, Sandra will be fine once we're back in the campervan, won't you, love?"

"I suppose so. We don't want to hold you up, Inspector. Will you keep us informed during the investigation?"

"As much as I can. We'll be doing our very best as a team to bring the person who did this to justice."

"Good, I hate the thought of another family going through the range of emotions that are tearing us apart right now."

Sara and Carla led the way up the corridor to the reception area. Mr and Mrs Holt shook their hands and said farewell.

"Such a friendly couple. My heart goes out to them," Sara said.

They climbed the stairs to the office.

"Hard one to deal with, losing your daughter in such circumstances. Is it worth speaking to the boyfriend?" Carla said.

Sara stopped mid-step. "What are you saying?"

"I'm just thinking if we're leaning towards the same person carrying out both murders in the village, how likely is it going to be the boyfriend? Unless he thought Victoria and the vicar were having an affair, I can't see why he would bump the pair of them off."

"Who knows what goes on at a parish council meeting behind closed doors?"

"Don't. That's got my thoughts churning."

They laughed and continued on their journey.

"We'll have a quick coffee and get on the road."

"I'll have a brief trawl through his social media accounts first, see if there's anything highlighted on there."

"Good idea. I'll see how the rest of the team is getting on in the meantime."

HALF AN HOUR LATER, Sara and Carla had pulled up outside Connors' flat.

"What's the betting he's not in?" Carla said.

"If he's not, didn't you say he worked at Bedford Garage?"

"That's right."

"Then we'll see him there. Let's try the home address first." Sara rang the bell but, as expected, there was no answer. "Off to Bedford Garage then."

They returned to the car and drove ten minutes to the garage on the other side of the town.

There were three cars on the forecourt, and when they entered the workshop, four mechanics were working on different cars inside. The nearest mechanic asked if he could help.

Sara smiled. "We're looking for Justin Connors. Is he around?"

"He's nipped out for a second or two, only to pick up some milk from the Co-op. I'd tell you to wait in his office, except he hates people being in there when he's not around."

"No problem. We'll stand over here, out of the way, until he comes back."

A man in beige chinos and a white shirt entered the garage carrying some milk. Sara took a punt it was him, and they stepped out of the shadows. His eyes narrowed immediately.

"I can smell coppers a mile off. I'm right, aren't I?"

Sara flashed her warrant card at him. "DI Sara Ramsey and DS Carla Jameson. Are you Justin Connors?"

"Yep, what about it?"

"We'd like a private chat with you, if that's all right?"

"Not really. We're up to our necks in it around here as it is. Can't this wait?"

"We can either chat here or ask you to accompany us down to the station. The choice is yours."

"Jesus, you lot are like dogs with bones, all of you. Come into my office then, and no, I won't be apologising for the mess in there. I'm in the middle of doing my end-of-year accounts, hence me going to fetch some milk. I'm in dire need of a coffee."

"Don't mind us. Hopefully, we'll be out of your hair soon enough."

"Is that a promise?" He didn't wait for a response.

They followed him into what could only be described as the after-effects of a tornado.

"You weren't joking," Sara quipped.

"It's the best I can do in an office this size. I'd invite you to take a seat, but there isn't a spare one."

"Don't worry, we can stand."

"So, go on then, I'm dying to know what all this is about."

"We'd like to know if you've seen your ex-girlfriend lately."

"Doh! Which one? I'm a good-looking lad, in case you haven't noticed. I've got dozens of exes."

He grinned, and Sara noticed he had a few gaps in his

teeth on the right-hand side. She couldn't help wondering what had happened to them.

Has another bloke punched his lights out over the years, or maybe Victoria put up a fight before she was killed, if he attacked and murdered her?

"Victoria Holt. I can tell by your expression her name rings a bell."

"Are you nuts? Of course it does. We were an item for about three years. Why, what's she had to say about our relationship?"

"Nothing. Have you seen her lately?"

"Not for a few months, and then we didn't speak to each other. I was out with my current girlfriend, and she was in town with a bunch of her friends. Why do you want to know?"

Sara found herself in a difficult situation. Did she tell him Victoria was dead or continue to ask questions in order to get a feel for their relationship from his point of view, bearing in mind what Victoria's parents had just told her?

"Has she texted or phoned you lately?"

"No, she wouldn't dare. If she came near me, Olivia would rip her to shreds. She's a feisty cow."

"I take it you mean your current girlfriend?"

"Yes, yes. Look, as you can see, I'm very busy, and I need to get all this shit over to my accountant by the end of the day, so can you get on with why you're here and bugger off? Sorry, I know that's not what you probably want to hear, but you can see for yourself what my life is like at the moment."

"Okay, we'd like to know where you were between the hours of six p.m. last night and seven a.m. this morning." Sara realised she hadn't received the time of death yet from Lorraine, so the time was a guess on her part.

"Bloody hell, now you're asking. I was here until eight last night, going through all this paperwork and putting it into the various files you see here, and then I stopped off at the pub for a couple of pints with Olivia. Why? If that bitch has told you otherwise, then she's an effing liar. Olivia is next door, if you don't believe me."

Sara's interest spiked. "Would it be possible for us to speak with Olivia?"

He tutted and heaved out a breath. "You guys are doing my head in. I need to get on with my work." He picked up the phone. "Olivia, if you've got a minute, can you pop in...? I know, tell me about it. Have you seen the state my office is in? Just get in here... you'll see for yourself soon enough." He slammed the phone down and shook his head. "Like I've already said, you couldn't have chosen a worse bloody day to show up."

"What do you want? Oh, sorry, I didn't know you had visitors." A brunette, wearing a black mini-skirt and a low-cut white top, appeared in the doorway behind them.

"I need you to tell these ladies where I was last night."

She frowned. "Is this some kind of trick question? Who are they?"

"They're coppers. Just tell them, and then they can leave us alone."

"He was with me."

"All night?" Sara pressed.

"Yes," Olivia said. She eyed Sara and Carla up and down, her nose screwed up, her distaste for them obvious. "Why? What's going on here? What are you accusing him of?"

"We haven't, not yet. Can you tell us at what time you left the garage?"

"I think it was at around eight, wasn't it, Justin?"

He nodded. "That's what I told them."

"And where did you go afterwards?" Sara asked. She had a sinking feeling they weren't going to get anywhere with this line of enquiry.

"We went to the pub. The White Swan is just down the road from our home. We had a few drinks and walked home; we picked up the cars on the way to work this morning."

"Thank you for verifying that. You're free to go."

"What? No, I demand to know what's going on here. If he's been up to something, then I need to know, and I believe you have a duty to tell me."

"Fucking charming, that is," Connors shouted. "I ain't been up to nothin'; nice of you to point the finger at me. If that's what you think of me, get out of my sight."

Olivia crossed her arms and stood her ground. "I'm not going anywhere, not until I know what this is all about." She glared at each of them as if emphasising her point.

"If you can corroborate his alibi, then there's nothing else for us to say."

"Wait a second, alibi for what?" Olivia screeched.

Sara glanced at Carla, who nodded. "Justin's ex-girlfriend, Victoria, umm… her body was found in a field close to the village where she lives."

"What the actual fuck?" Justin said. He jumped out of his seat and stomped over the papers on the floor to get to Sara. Carla blocked his path. "And you've come here today to accuse me of killing her, is that it?"

Sara pulled on her partner's arm. "It's okay, Carla, you don't have to protect me. If Mr Connors wants to express his anger, let him do it. He'll be banged up in a cell within half an hour."

"Bollocks to that. How the fuck do you expect me to react after hearing that?"

"Wait, why are you coming down heavily on Justin?" Olivia asked.

"Because of their history," Sara said.

Justin flung his arm up in the air. "That was before. I'm a

changed man, I tell you. Have I ever laid a hand on you in the time that I've known you, Olivia?"

"No, never." She gasped. "Don't tell me you used to hit her?"

He bowed his head in shame, then raised it and pleaded with his girlfriend. "I've told you, I'm a changed man. I would never lash out at you the way I did with her. She pushed my buttons more than once and drove me to the edge. You have no idea what I went through with her."

"You attacked another woman? I'm struggling to believe what I'm hearing here."

"Yes, but that relationship differed from what we have."

Olivia had clearly heard enough and marched off. Justin attempted to rush after her, but slid on the sheets of paper on the floor and ended up in a heap at Sara's feet.

"Are you all right?" Sara asked, sensing by his narked expression that he was about to erupt.

"A lot you care. You've done this intentionally. Come here to make a show of me, haven't you?"

"Not in the slightest. Sorry you feel that way. Do you need a hand getting up?"

His shoes struggled to get a grip, and he ended up clawing at the table to assist him. A door banged behind them, and Olivia walked past, wearing a long woollen coat, her handbag over her shoulder.

"Find someone else to fill my shoes, at home and at work. I don't have time for this shit. Once an abuser, always an abuser, in my experience. You ain't gonna get handy with your fists with me, got that, dickhead?"

"Olivia, come back. You can't walk out on me."

"Who says I can't? Watch me." Then she threw over her shoulder, "Ladies, you've done me a favour. I was getting bored with the prick, anyway. Have a great life, Justin. My stuff will be cleared out of the flat by the time you get home."

"Come back, Olivia. You can't walk out on me today of all days. You know how much I have to get through today. I need you."

"Tough shit. I don't associate with abusers, end of. Any bloke who lays a finger on a woman is an effing coward in my book."

"I'm not. I might have slipped up now and again a few years ago. Ah shit… what's the point? You weren't the only one getting bored, bitch."

"And there we have it, in front of all these witnesses, your true colours coming out."

"Yeah, cheap and nasty, like you."

Olivia stopped in her tracks and spun around to face him. She opened her mouth to speak and then shook her head. "You're not worth it. I think I've had a very lucky escape." Then she marched out of the workshop.

"Yeah, that makes two of us. Going back to Mummy's, are you? I'll be round later to pick the car up, or had you forgotten I paid for it?"

Olivia stormed back in and shouted, "You bastard! That's my car. You gave it to me as a gift for my birthday."

"Fuck off, you thought I did. It's still registered in my name." He laughed at her furious expression.

She flew at him and tried to get into the office, but Sara and Carla stood in her way.

"Now then, we'll have none of that, not while we're on site. You both need to calm down."

"Keep your nose out of it," Justin snarled, his lip curled up at the side. "All of this is down to you. You come in here, stirring it, and expect people to carry on with their days as if nothing has happened."

"That wasn't our intention at all. We're investigating a serious crime, dealing with a murder inquiry. All we're doing is our job. Your reaction has justified us visiting you today."

"What are you saying? That you had me at the top of your suspect list?"

Sara nodded. "Yes, can you blame us after hearing about your relationship with Victoria?"

"It was a mistake. She walked away, and I haven't really seen her since, apart from the odd occasion."

"And we believe you. If Olivia hadn't backed up your alibi, it would have been a different story entirely."

"Great. Glad you believe me, eventually. After my girl-friend dumped me and walked out, leaving me without a bloody secretary. I'm going to complain about you showing up here today with the specific intention of accusing me of Victoria's murder. I'm gobsmacked that anyone could ever think that I would go to such lengths as taking someone's life."

"Feel free to put a complaint in. In our defence, I think you'll find we have the right to question anyone connected with the victim, who has either said or made any threats against them in the past, therefore, I believe the Independent Office for Police Conduct will come down in our favour."

"We'll see about that. Are we done here?"

"We are. Thank you for your time. Would it be all right if we have a quick word with your staff?"

His arms flew out to the sides. "Are you kidding me? What the fuck for? Can't you see how busy they are?"

"Just doing our duty."

He shook his head in disgust and peered over his shoulder at the paperwork covering every surface of his office. "Do what you frigging want. I've got work to do."

Sara and Carla stepped out of the office. Connors slammed the door behind them then let out a frustrated expletive that was heard by everyone in the building, judging by the way the other staff members turned their way.

"Hi, guys, we're going to talk to you individually. Nothing

to be worried about, but we're entitled to question you as part of our investigation," Sara announced and approached the first mechanic. "I'm DI Sara Ramsey, and this is my partner, DS Carla Jameson, and your name is?"

"Bob Davis. What's this all about? We heard snippets of your conversation with the boss and saw Olivia walk out."

"It's unfortunate that happened. Do you know Victoria Holt?"

He frowned. "I don't think so, should I?"

"She used to live with Justin before Olivia came along, I believe."

"Oh, yeah, Victoria, yes, she came here once or twice. Haven't seen her around, not since they split up. Is she the one who's dead? I heard you say you're conducting a murder inquiry."

"Sadly, yes. Has Justin ever mentioned her since they split up?"

"Never, or should I say, not to my knowledge."

"Thanks for speaking with us."

They moved around the room to the next three mechanics and asked the same questions; their answers were the same as Bob's.

Sara and Carla left the garage and returned to the car.

Sitting behind the steering wheel, Sara leaned forward and rested her forehead against it. "Give me strength, if not that, then please give us a sign of where to look next to find the bloody killers."

"Hey, what's all this? Stop doubting yourself. Something will come our way soon. I know it will."

Sara sat up and smiled at her partner. "I suppose it's back to square one for us. We have a list of parishioners we need to question. We've let that slip and we might be missing a trick."

"Well, let's face it, it's not like we're inundated with options, is it?"

CHAPTER 5

The killers waited for their next victim, Parry, in the car park across the road from the council chambers in Hereford.

"He's taking his time. It's already six o'clock."

"He'll be out soon. Stop fretting," the driver said. He was also feeling anxious about the wait, but knew how important it was for them to remain calm. In his experience, very little was achieved when anxiety was a dominant emotion.

His statement resulted in several minutes of his accomplice sighing. He tapped his fingers on the steering wheel and then gripped it firmly when their target appeared, except he wasn't alone.

"Shit! Not what we need. We're going to have to follow them."

"He might be walking her to her car. They seem pretty friendly. Did I just see her hand brush against his?"

The driver scowled. "I missed it. I wouldn't put it past him, though. He looks like a real slimeball. We'd better put our masks on."

They slipped them on and sank low in their seats as the

couple passed their vehicle and entered his car a few rows behind them.

"Oh my God, he's all over her, and that's definitely not his wife. I carried out some research on him earlier. What the heck is he playing at?"

"I think that's obvious, don't you?"

The couple separated, and Parry started the car. He exited the car park, and the killers followed him at a safe distance.

"I wonder where they're going."

"My guess is we're about to find out," the driver said.

They approached a roundabout, and he let two cars go in front of him to avoid Parry suspecting he was being followed. Mind you, with the stunner sitting next to him, he'd probably be too distracted to notice, anyway.

"It'll be interesting to see where he takes her, especially as he's well-known in the area. What a prick! Why do men do that? Cheat on their bloody wives."

"Wanting their cake and eating it comes to mind."

Parry drove five miles out of town and then entered a country lane that was barely wide enough for a tractor to use. The killers drove past and pulled into the lay-by up the road and waited for Parry to reappear.

"I don't think we'll be waiting long. He doesn't seem the type to keep it up for over two minutes," the driver said, and they both laughed.

"I knew a man like that once upon a time."

The driver faced his accomplice. "Are you referring to… It doesn't matter, I'd rather not know."

"The answer to your question is, yes. Shame on him. He was a sly bugger, too, always going off with other women."

"Oh no, this isn't the time for us to be holding this type of conversation. We'll discuss it later."

"I'd rather not. I'm just saying…"

"Well, don't. I could do without the distraction." He kept a close eye on his rear-view mirror and spotted the rear end of Parry's vehicle backing onto the main road. A couple of cars passed by and beeped their horns. "What a prat. I guess he had more important things on his mind rather than how he was going to reverse out onto a main road at this time of night."

"That'll teach him, eh? Cheating bastard deserves all he gets from us later."

"Keep that anger flowing. You'll need it for when we do the deed."

"Don't worry, it's been ebbing and flowing for days."

After several failed attempts, Parry successfully reversed and put his foot down before two more cars came whizzing past.

"Hold on, I'm going to use these two to shield us. The next car is way back, so I need to take the chance now."

"It's a fast road. You'd better put your foot down if you want to keep up with him."

"Keep an eye on his vehicle from your side. Let me know if he indicates left."

"Will do."

Their journey took them out towards Wilton, but stopped a few miles short of where the other murders had taken place.

"That's strange, he lives around here... don't tell me she's a bloody neighbour of his."

"What the fuck? This is going to scupper our plans tonight."

"Don't lose hope, not yet. We're still about ten minutes from his house."

"He's turning left!" the passenger shouted excitedly.

"All right, stay calm. I think this is a dead end. I'm going to stay here for a few minutes until he comes back out."

"If he comes out. What if we've got this all wrong?"

"A quick shag up a country lane and then home to his wife for dinner. I don't think so."

They parked behind a car within spitting distance of the road Parry had taken. He reappeared several minutes later and took a right back onto the main road again.

"Now we can make our move. His house is about three minutes from here. Be prepared."

"I'm prepared, don't worry." The passenger collected the crowbar from between the seats.

"I like your thinking. Hold tight. I'm going to make my move while the traffic is light."

He drove up behind Parry and swerved around him. Moments later, he braked and angled the van across the road, blocking Parry's path. The councillor slammed on the brakes, and several skid marks later, he drew his car to a halt and switched off his engine. Then his car door flew open, and he marched towards their van. It was dark by now, so Parry wouldn't have seen the killers or been aware that they were wearing masks.

The driver jumped out, ready for the confrontation, but it never came, because as soon as Parry realised what was going on, he tried to leg it back to his car.

The driver ran after him, caught him by the scruff and, with Parry's arms flailing, he dragged him back to the van. The passenger got out and slammed the crowbar into Parry's stomach, winding him. This allowed them to easily manoeuvre him.

"We're going to need to knock him out and tie him up."

The crowbar came down on his head and knocked Parry out cold. "I'll get the rope. There's a sack in the back as well."

"Good thinking. Hurry, before another car comes this way."

The exercise was carried out swiftly, and then the driver moved Parry's vehicle to the side of the road, parking it slightly on the grass verge. Then he ran back and helped to bundle Parry into the back of the van. Together, they bound his feet and his hands, placed the sack over his head, and laid him down.

"The location isn't far from here. Ray said I could use one of his barns at the other end of his farm for a while. I've told him I'm working on a secret project and not to go up there."

"I hope you can trust him."

"I can. I went to school with him. He's busy at this time of year, tending to his animals, preparing for the winter."

"Good, because I'd hate to have all our efforts unravel before our mission is completed."

"You worry too much. Get in." He drove the couple of miles up the road to the location. The barn was perfect for what they had in mind. "We'll get him comfortable and leave him overnight to stew, then I'll come back first thing to feed and water him."

"I wouldn't bother. I'd let the fucker starve if it were down to me, cheating bastard."

"A tad harsh. We'll do it my way. It's more humane."

"On one proviso."

"What's that?" The driver scanned the area, looking for somewhere suitable to put their hostage. There was a screened-off area over to the right, where the bales of hay were piled high. If Ray stuck his head in for a sneaky peek, hopefully Parry wouldn't be seen.

"That I kill him."

"Whatever, it makes no odds to me. I want him to suffer for a few days first. We'll remove the hood and put some tape over his mouth to keep him quiet."

"If you think that will do the trick."

"Do you have doubts about that?"

His accomplice shrugged. "I have doubts about this whole

setup. If I had my way, he'd be strung up from that beam and left to suffer, to die a slow death."

"I've got news for you. That method isn't a slow death."

"Then we need to think of something else. He deserves to suffer a lot before he dies."

"I hear you. Let's get him prepared for now, and we'll discuss the ins and outs of how we punish him, later."

They dragged Parry's body behind the stack of hay, secured his arms to a post, removed the hood, and placed a large strip of tape over his mouth.

"That's perfect." The driver kicked Parry's leg to wake him up. "Wakey-wakey, tosspot."

After another couple of well-aimed kicks to the man's shins and then his thighs, Parry stirred and moaned. Realising the trouble he was in, he stared up at them, his eyes almost bulging out of their sockets. He tried to speak, but the thickness of the tape kept him quiet.

"Shocked, are you? I bet you didn't think your day would end up like this, right?"

He squirmed, trying to break free of his constraints, but stopped after a few seconds, realising it was pointless. He tried to communicate, but they ignored him and walked out of the barn. The driver switched off the light and craned his neck to hear.

He could tell Parry was in complete panic mode. "A good way to end our evening."

They laughed and returned to the van.

THE FOLLOWING DAY, on his way to work, the driver stopped off at the barn. He set the carrier bag down beside Parry, who had dark shadows under his eyes. "I hope you slept well?"

Parry shook his head and tried to speak.

"Hush now. All in good time. Now, this is what's going to happen: one false move on your part, and I'll have no hesitation in killing you, just like the vicar and Victoria."

Parry's eyes widened again.

"That's right, we're the ones responsible for their deaths. Now then, I'm going to remove the tape. Any noise from you, and I'll kill you instantly, not that anyone would hear you way out here. Just to make you aware, we're in the middle of nowhere. Are you going to behave?"

Parry's head bobbed up and down.

"Good. I stopped off at the garage and bought you a sandwich. Cheese and ham, tough shit if you don't like that combination." He removed the sandwich from the bag together with a bottle of water he'd picked up as well and put them on the floor beside Parry. "This is probably going to hurt." He ripped the tape from Parry's mouth.

"Why are you doing this to me? I have done nothing wrong."

Under his mask, the driver cocked an eyebrow. "Don't play the fucking innocent with me, mate. You're a councillor, a corrupt one at that."

"How dare you call me that? What proof have you got?"

"Hey, you're in no position to shout the odds at me, got that?" The driver held his hand flat and then jabbed Parry in the stomach with his stiffened fingers.

The hostage cried out in pain. "Please, you've got this all wrong. I have done nothing."

"Bollocks. I know differently. I've been observing you for months, meeting up with different people in this community, mainly business owners and farmers. Each time you pocket an envelope full of cash."

"That's slander. I've done nothing of the sort. Prove it."

"The thing is, I have enough proof to show the authorities and put you away. However, I also know you of old. You'll come up with an abundance of lies that will probably get you off the hook. Now, are you going to eat this or not?"

"Not. I'd rather starve than take food from you. You're wrong about me. Give me the chance to prove it."

"Tut-tut, you should never refuse food from someone keeping you hostage. You never know when the next meal is going to come your way."

"I don't care about the food; all I want to do is clear my name."

"It's not going to happen. I have the proof… actually, I've got it here. We'll take a look at it together. Yes, let's do that." He removed his mobile from his jacket pocket and scrolled through to a video he'd made recently. He'd filmed Parry at a secret location where he'd met up with Ralph Windsor, the farmer who was causing a lot of problems for the residents of Wilton. "Here you go. Tell me I'm wrong after viewing the evidence."

Parry watched the video of himself chatting conspiratori-ally with Watson, both men periodically sneaking a peek over their shoulders before the farmer handed over a large, stuffed envelope. At this point, the camera zoomed in to focus on Parry, checking the contents of the package in his possession. He then smiled and shook the farmer's hand. Both men parted and left the area in their respective vehicles.

"Caught in the act! You're going to have a hard time denying that to the authorities, and that's not the only piece of evidence I will upload to the internet this evening. I have you bang to rights on five different videos. Are you still going to tell me you're innocent because the proof is telling me otherwise?"

"All right, all right, I admit it. Please, if you let me go, I promise not to tell the police about you abducting me, and I'll give you fifty grand as well."

"Fifty grand, eh? Is that how much Windsor has given you?"

"Is it, heck? Don't be ridiculous."

"Then why pluck that particular sum out of the air?"

"Because I value my life."

"Fifty grand, is that all you're worth? It's not that generous, mate."

"Jesus, I can't win, can I?"

"Ah, it's finally dawning on you. Nope, no sum of money is going to change my mind about you. You're a cheating, corrupt bastard through and through, and yes, we were following you last night when you pulled over for a quick shag with that blonde."

"She's my secretary. I was giving her a lift home, that's all. We stopped off to go over a plan I have in mind for how to set up our office."

He howled with laughter. "Pull the other one, you lying tosser. Let's see what other footage I can show you. Ah, yes, this is another good one you should see."

It showed Parry arriving at a remote location on the edge of a forest. He exited the vehicle and ventured into the trees, where he met up with another man, unaware they had been followed and were being filmed. The same thing happened: the stranger passed over an overstuffed envelope, and Parry checked the contents before they shook hands and returned to their cars.

"What have you got to say for yourself?"

"Nothing. He's a pal of mine who owed me some money. We agreed to meet up in the woods. He goes there all the time to walk his dog."

"Funny, I can't see a dog on the footage."

"He was off, sniffing around in the undergrowth."

"Whose side do you think the public will come down on, once this comes out?"

Parry swallowed and tears welled up. "Please, you can't do this. It's going to ruin me. I've worked for twenty years to get to where I am today. Don't let a few video clips spoil what I've achieved in that time."

"Are you for real? You're even more twisted than I've given you credit for. The public are the losers because of your corruption and willingness to bend the rules for bastards like Windsor, who think nothing about lining your pockets."

Parry stared at him. "I'm sorry."

"Words are cheap. You're not sorry at all. You've ruined so many lives throughout the years, and you couldn't give a toss as long as you keep taking the backhanders."

"I'll stop doing it. Yes, I'll promise to do that, if you let me go."

"Not a cat in hell's chance. We're going to punish you, put you through hell... I like that word. It's the second time I've used it in as many seconds because that is going to be your destination by the time we've finished with you."

Parry's mouth opened, and his lips trembled. "I don't want to die."

The driver leaned in closer and whispered, "I've got news for you. None of us do, but shit happens. We all have to go sometime."

"Are you sure there's nothing I can do to persuade you?"

"Nothing! Your fate is going to be in our hands when the time comes. When that's going to be, well, we're not sure about that yet. It might be tomorrow or the next day, or we might even be tempted to keep you here for a week or more. That decision will depend on how much you piss me off in the meantime."

"I don't know what you expect or want from me. I repeat, I've done nothing wrong. Those videos prove zilch."

A sudden idea sparked in his mind. He searched Parry's

pockets, annoyed he hadn't already thought about taking the man's mobile from him when they'd originally left him. "Got a banking app, have you?"

"Yes, I have. I can transfer enough funds for you; it'll transfer right away, and then you can set me free."

He played along with Parry long enough to get the phone open and for him to tell him the password for his bank account. He grinned when the man's bank statement appeared on the tiny screen. Scrolling through it, he felt the anger rise. Foolishly, he believed he would see the proof with his own eyes on the mobile.

"I'm an idiot. As if you'd deposit all the dodgy money you've taken as backhanders in your bank account. It's probably shoved in a safe at home, isn't it? Maybe we'll go there tonight. Force your wife to open it."

"You'll be wasting your time. My wife doesn't know the combination to the safe. You're going to need to take me with you."

"You sound so cocksure of yourself, and you can get that smug grin off your face. FYI, there's more than one way to get into a safe."

"I'd like to see you try."

"That's the thing. You won't be around to see anything soon enough." He laughed and replaced the tape over Parry's mouth. "You had your chance to eat and drink. It's your loss. I'm off to do my day job now. No idea what time I'll be back tonight or if I'll even bother coming back. I might even decide to pay your missus a call, see if she's lonely, if you know what I mean? What with you dipping your wick elsewhere."

Parry wrestled with his bindings, trying to get to him as the anger blazed in his eyes.

The driver wet his forefinger, stroked it in the air and walked out of the barn.

CHAPTER 6

*W*e haven't really established a connection between the two victims other than they were members of the local parish council and they lived in the same village," Sara announced at the morning meeting the next day. "After we visited Victoria's boyfriend yesterday, he was shocked to hear of her demise and, although he abused her when they were living together, I can't see him being involved in her death."

"Where does that leave us, then?" Carla said.

Sara took a sip of her coffee. "Going through the list of attendees at the church the evening Paul Gains was killed. I know we got distracted when the second victim surfaced, but it's all we have at present. Especially as nothing has come up via the research, the rest of the team has carried out in our absence."

"What if the couple were having an affair?" Jill said.

"My gut is telling me that's unlikely, but we can see what the people attending the church that evening have to say first and go from there. We're going to do this as a team. Sorry, Jill, if you can stay here to man the phones, the rest of us will go through the list and see what we can come up with this morning."

"What about the parish council angle?" Craig asked.

"Let's go back to the list of the attendees at the church meeting for now and revisit the parish council side of things later. For all we know, Victoria might have been there that evening, even though her name wasn't on the list. That's another question we can ask during the interviews. Right, is there anything else you can think of that we should cover?"

The team all shook their heads.

"Sup up then, and let's get on the road."

"Sorry, I've thought of something," Carla said.

"What's that?"

"Well, Victoria was a mobile hairdresser with a distinctive car. What if she witnessed what happened to Gains, and the killers tracked her down to ensure she didn't speak?"

Sara mulled over her partner's suggestion for a second or two. "That's a workable proposition and could be the answer we're searching for."

TWENTY MINUTES LATER, after Sara had divided the list up and given the relevant names to the team members, they set off back to the village.

Sara and Carla stopped off at Katherine Tinder's bungalow first.

The lady came to the door aided by a walking stick. "Hello, can I help you?"

Sara produced her warrant card. "Hello, Mrs Tinder, I'm DI Sara Ramsey, and this is my partner, DS Carla Jameson. I wonder if we might come in and speak with you for a moment or two."

"I've been expecting someone to call. Don't mind me, I took a tumble yesterday; the stick was my husband's. I dug it out last night and I'm using it as a precaution. I can't get an appointment to see the doctor until next week. It'll probably be better by then."

"Are you all right? It looks painful," Sara said as they followed her into a spacious lounge.

"It catches me out now and again. Definitely easier with the stick than without it. What can I do for you?"

"We're going through the list of attendees for the meeting that was held at the church the night Paul Gains was killed."

Katherine's eyes watered, and her chin dipped to her chest. "I don't think I'll ever get over losing our dear vicar. He was one of the nicest men I've ever known, the total opposite of our last vicar, who always remained distant from his parishioners. Paul was so open and welcoming; he had a cheeky side to him, too. He was always smiling, had a thoughtful nature, if that doesn't sound too silly. I'd say he showed the human kindness that is so often missing in today's society. I don't think that had anything to do with him being a man of the cloth, either."

"You're not the first person to tell us that. Hard to believe someone would go out of their way to kill him. Perhaps you wouldn't mind going over what happened at the church that evening?"

"Of course. I'm the organist at the church. I was sorting out which tunes would be suitable for the Christmas Service that is coming up. Paul and I came to the agreement that we wanted something different this year and agreed on several interesting pieces. In that respect, it was a successful evening. We spoke about that and our families on the way home."

"You walked home with him?"

"That's right, my leg was fine then, although we had trouble battling the wind and rain at times." She smiled as she obviously remembered the evening with fondness. "He said to me, 'Come on, Katherine, let's put our best foot forward'." She shook her head as the smile slipped. "Such a nice man. I still can't believe I will never see him again. A character so full of life."

"Try not to get upset."

"It's very difficult not to when someone like that is taken from us."

"I know. I'm truly sorry for the community's loss. We're trying to piece together his last movements that night. So he saw you to your door. After that, was he returning to the church or heading home?"

"Straight home. We'd finished at the church, and he was going home to his lovely wife. I keep wanting to go over there, to reach out to her, but I know what it's like to lose someone dear to you. Initially, you just want to shut the world out and reflect on the good times you've had with that person. Once this first phase has ended, she's going to need the people of this community to rally around for her, and they will. We're a good bunch. I have to ask how Danny is coping with his father's death."

"We're not entirely sure would be the honest answer. Yvonne's sister travelled from Worcester to help out. I'm not sure precisely how long she stayed or whether she returned home after a few hours. Has everyone in the family slotted into the village, like Paul?"

"Oh yes, we all adore Danny and Yvonne. I know their son has health problems, but he's also got a heart of gold, just like his father had."

Sara felt she could neither agree nor disagree because she hadn't been with Danny much when they'd visited the house. She went over to the bay window and glanced out at the street. "You can't see the vicarage from here. Did you notice anyone hanging around while you walked home?"

"No, nothing, but then Paul and I were concentrating on keeping ourselves dry and getting home quickly. The weather was atrocious. Had it been that bad earlier, I would have stayed home. I think a lot of us would."

"Understandable. What about during the evening, back at the church, did Paul have any disagreements with anyone?"

"Gracious me, no, definitely not. Anyone who knows him well would pour water on that suggestion. Paul never fell out or got angry with people. It wasn't in him to do it."

"What I meant was, did anyone pick an argument with him, perhaps?"

She paused to contemplate and then shook her head. "No, not that I can think of. It was a pleasant evening all around. We had a few laughs here and there when Sid found some costumes out the back and started playing the fool with them."

"Sid?"

"An old-timer who helps at the church. He keeps the graves tidy, all voluntarily, because that's the type of man he is. Everyone is the same. We're all keen to help in the village."

"And it's genuinely a nice place to live?"

"Absolutely, apart from that smell and disruption from the farm we've had to contend with for a while."

Sara inclined her head. "Where's the farm located?"

"At the bottom of the hill. There was a public meeting about it the night after Paul died. I didn't attend because I'd had my fall. But a few of the locals rang me and told me it was a waste of time going because the farmer brought all his friends along to speak up for him. The parish council don't care, some of them don't even live here."

"Wasn't Paul on the parish council?"

"Yes, I think he would have made a difference had he been there, but maybe not. We believe there is more going on at that farm than meets the eye."

"Thanks for letting us know; we'll add it to our list, ensure we have a word with the farmer."

"I wish someone in authority would because the Environmental Health and the Planning Department don't appear to want to know."

Sara's mind went back to another case they'd had to deal with recently, involving a dubious EH officer. Could there be a link? The officer was currently serving time in prison for being in cahoots with a different farmer on the other side of the city.

"Boss? Are you all right?" Carla nudged her knee.

"Sorry, yes, just caught up in my thoughts. Is there anything else going on in the village that we should know about, Katherine?"

"I don't think so. Are you sure you're okay, dear? You seem a little peaky."

Sara waved the woman's concern away. "I'm fine. Don't worry about me. We'll be off now then. We've got several people we need to speak to in the village. I'm going to leave you one of my cards. Please call me if you think of anything else we should know."

"I will do." Katherine struggled to get out of her chair.

"No, stay there. We'll close the door behind us."

"If you're sure. It was nice meeting you. I hope you find the person responsible for killing Paul, soon."

"I'm sure we will. Silly me, yes, there is something else... can you tell me if Victoria Holt was at the church the evening Paul was killed?"

Katherine remained silent as she thought. After a slight pause, she replied, "No, I don't think I saw her there. Why?"

Sara cringed; it was obvious that Katherine wasn't aware of the latest victim's death. "Sorry to be the bearer of bad news, but Victoria's body was also found in a field a few days ago."

"Oh no. How did she die? Or can't you tell me that?"

"She was murdered, the same as Paul."

"Goodness me. Are you telling me the murders are connected?"

"Possibly. We've yet to find a connection between the two victims other than they lived in the village and were both members of the parish council."

"My, oh my, what is this world coming to? I'm truly shocked by this news. We've never had any problems of this magnitude in the village before."

"Try not to let it unsettle you. We have a police presence in the village and will continue to patrol the area for another few days. I'll make sure of that."

"Thank you. It is more than a little disconcerting to think there might be a killer either living in the village or coming here to pick off the residents."

"I'm sorry, I shouldn't have told you."

"No, I'm glad you have. It must be a nightmare for you to investigate two murders instead of just the one. I didn't really know Victoria that well. I hear she was a good hairdresser; my neighbour Doreen used her all the time."

"Which side?" Sara thumbed left and right.

"This side, on the right."

"Thanks again, Katherine."

"I don't know why you're thanking me. It's not like I've told you anything of use, is it?"

"Thanks for speaking with us. You take care of that leg of yours. If it's still giving you problems in a few hours, make sure you get yourself off to the A and E Department."

"I will, I promise."

Sara and Carla waved at the older woman and left the house.

"Sweet lady, so cut up about the vicar," Carla noted as Sara closed the door behind them.

"Hard to handle for the older residents. Isn't there a Doreen on our list?"

Carla flipped her notebook open. "Doreen Corker, and yes, she lives next door."

"Nice and convenient. We'll take that rather than trudging from one end of the village to the other."

"Wait, can I have a word with you first?"

Sara stopped walking and faced her. "Is something wrong?"

"I don't know, is it? You drifted off in there, Katherine and I both noticed it. What was that all about?"

"Sorry, you're right, I did. Something just struck me as soon as Katherine mentioned the Environmental Health was not doing their job properly."

Carla tutted and clicked her fingers. "I'm with you. The case we solved where the farmer was harassing the residents in the new builds on the other side of the city. What are you thinking? That there might be something dubious going on again?"

Sara shrugged. "I don't know. It's a possibility, I suppose." She scratched her head and sighed. "Or is that case too familiar and leading me to think there might be a similarity in the investigations?"

Carla held her arms out to the sides and hitched up her shoulders. "I don't know. It might be worth us exploring, especially if the EH Department has already had one corrupt officer imprisoned."

"Definitely worth us investigating. I think it would be remiss of us not to." Sara removed her phone from her pocket and dialled the station. "Jill, it's me. Can you do me a favour?"

"Of course. Name it, boss."

"See what you can find out for me about a farm in Wilton village causing a disruption, if you would? One resident has informed me that there was a public meeting held regarding the smell and noise coming from the property. She also told us that the authorities, namely the Environmental Health, have been worse than useless in dealing with the problem and the complaints."

"Oh bugger, not again. Let me do some digging and get back to you."

"Great. We're going to continue interviewing people on the list. Good luck." She ended the call feeling more positive than she had about the investigation so far.

"Well, that's lightened your steps, hasn't it?" Carla said.

"You could say that."

They entered the next garden, and Sara knocked on the neighbour's door. A woman in her seventies, or maybe eighties, answered it. Sara introduced herself and Carla, and the woman instantly invited them in.

"Shocking what has been going on in the village. First the vicar, and now my sweet hairdresser. Do you have any idea who has killed these decent people?"

"Not yet. My team is interviewing throughout the village, asking people if they saw anything the night the vicar was killed."

"I didn't, not a thing. Wasn't that the night the bad weather hit us?"

"That's right."

"I battened down the hatches that night and went to bed early with a book."

"Perhaps you can tell us more about Victoria?"

"She's been cutting my hair for over five years now, maybe longer. You know how time flies when you're least expecting it to."

"I do. Did she have a lot of clients in the village?"

"Yes, she was very popular. I don't know what I'm going to do without her. Sandra and John must be feeling devastated, too.

"Yes, I had to ask them to cut short their holiday and return to the area so that I could share the news with them."

"Oh no, they do like their time away in their campervan. I'm not surprised they came back, though. Their daughter meant the world to them."

"They've got a tough few days ahead of them. When was the last time you spoke to Victoria?"

"She visited me at the end of last week. I used to enjoy my chats with her. She was always very attentive, one of the best hairdressers I've had over the years."

"We're more interested in her role with the parish council. Did she ever tell you about that?"

"Off and on. She didn't confide in me or break any confidences, but she told me that the meetings can get a bit heated now and again."

Sara sat forward on the edge of the sofa, eager to learn more. "Can you give us an example?"

"No, not really. She never gave any details but often said the monthly meetings periodically divided the members."

"Was she close to Paul Gains, the vicar?"

"I'm aware of who he is, or should I say, was. You're testing me there, dear. I wouldn't like to say, I suppose she must have been if they were on the council together. I'm sorry, that's as much as I can tell you."

Sensing they wouldn't get much further, Sara smiled and rose to her feet. "Thank you for seeing us. We'd better get on. We have a lot of people to interview."

"I apologise for not being more helpful, but I tend to keep myself to myself these days."

"There's no need. I quite understand. Take care of yourself."

. . .

145

THE REST of the morning was spent knocking on doors and listening to the same information. Sara's frustration grew with every villager they met. She kept in regular contact with the other team members, and they pretty much had the same results. At twelve-forty-five, she decided enough was enough, and they all returned to the station. Sara stopped off at the baker's down the road and bought sandwiches and cakes for all of them.

Over lunch, they dissected the information they had sourced, which just about filled a third of an A4 page—very disappointing indeed.

Jill raised her hand. "Do you want to hear what I've discovered, boss?"

"Yes, go on, make my day, Jill. I think we could all do with cheering up."

She laughed. "No pressure then. I searched online for the planning proposals that have been submitted for Windsor's farm. There was plenty for me to sift through over the past two years since he bought it. The latest one is a retrospective planning application for a change of use to one of the barns. I then went to the parish council's website, and apparently, they announced there would be a public meeting to discuss the issues they were having at the farm. That meeting took place the night after Paul Gains was killed."

"I'm aware of that meeting. I believe Mrs Tinder mentioned it. What about the Environmental Health? Is there anything showing up around them?"

"I found an article in the local paper in which one resident had complained about the smell emanating from the farm and citing the disruption that had occurred in the village over the past few years. An EH officer by the name of Nick Baines said that they took every complaint seriously, and they were in constant contact with the farmer."

"Okay, it might be worth us speaking with this Nick

Baines, and the farmer, for that matter. I'd also like to find out who the other members of the parish council are; is there a head councillor? I'm not sure, I've never had to deal with a Parish Council before. Jill, can you find that out for me?"

"I've got the information up on my screen now, boss. It was the last place I looked. There are four members, two of whom are already dead: Paul Gains and Victoria Holt."

"Okay, let's see what we can find out about the others, just in case that's the reason the victims were targeted."

"What about the farmer?" Carla asked.

"Let's keep a close eye on him for now. Craig and Barry, fancy doing some surveillance work for me?"

Craig, as eager as a pup, jumped out of his seat. "I'm up for it."

"All right, calm down. What about you, Barry?"

"I suppose so. How long for, boss? Because I've got to be somewhere this evening. Gemma has been given some tickets for the theatre."

Sara cocked an eyebrow. "That'll be nice for you. Just until the end of your shift. How's that? I think it's the only way we're going to get a sense of what's going on down there."

Once they'd eaten their lunch, the two men left the office.

"Let's keep digging, peeps. I need to chase up a couple of PMs from Lorraine. She's being really slack this week. Oops, did I say that out loud? Ignore me."

Sara rang the pathologist, but she was preoccupied, dealing with Victoria Holt's parents. Sara left a message with one tech, asking for Lorraine to call her back, and then got on with the paperwork she hadn't had time to tackle first thing.

CHAPTER 7

They returned to the barn to find Parry staring at them wide-eyed, slumped against his restraints.

"Have you been a good boy while we've been away?" the driver said. He noted the drink he'd left had been knocked over, but the sandwich was still in the same place. "Now, are you going to eat this or not? It's the only food we'll be offering you today."

Parry shook his head and said something neither of them caught behind the tape.

The driver removed it, but added a warning. "Shout out and you'll be punished, got that?"

Parry nodded. "Please, why are you doing this to me?"

"You know why. You should stop asking dumb questions. Has anyone been here today in our absence?"

"No, no one. Please, I have money, lots of it. I'll give it to you willingly if you'll let me go. I don't want to be here, not like this."

"There's a surprise. I don't suppose anyone appreciates their dismal surroundings when they're being held hostage."

"What do you want from me?"

148

"Truth be told, nothing. We're going to play a little game with you now."

"What game? I don't like games, never have done."

The masked couple laughed.

"Get him," his accomplice said. "Like he has a choice."

The driver replaced the tape over Parry's mouth, sick of the sound of his voice, and opened the holdall they'd brought with them. He withdrew a hammer and tapped it on Parry's right knee, just a gentle tap, to gauge his reaction. Parry squirmed, which only added to the driver's annoyance. Then, with their gazes locked, he brought the hammer down heavily on his knee. Parry cried out, but the tape muted his words. Without hesitation, he smashed Parry's left knee as well. Then the driver removed a hacksaw from his holdall and placed it over Parry's left ankle while his associate held his foot in place. With each movement of the blade going back and forth over his bones, Parry's eyes widened more, and his muffled screams came thick and fast.

"I'm enjoying this. Maybe now he'll understand what torture he's put our village through. Sitting there throughout the meetings with a smug grin stretched across his face." His attention switched back to Parry. "You sicken us. You've got no respect for the residents at all. Mind you, it says a lot about a man's character when he gives his secretary a lift home and stops off for a five-minute shag en route."

Parry's ligaments snapped. The accomplice took the pressure off the foot, and it flopped to an uncomfortable angle. The driver carried out the same process on the other ankle. Tears streamed down Parry's cheeks. At one point, he actually passed out because of the intense pain, but the driver poured water over his face to revive him. With the second foot hanging on by a thread, they untied one of his hands, and the accomplice gripped his fingers. Parry did his best to get away, but the hammer came out of the bag again and was smashed against one of his shins.

"Behave, or it'll get worse. What am I saying? Just behave and accept your punishment. We're going to show you what a worthless piece of shit you truly are."

The torture continued until Parry couldn't stand it any longer and he passed out. This time they decided not to revive him and instead untied him and carried him outside, where they put him in the back of the van.

"What are we going to do with him now?"

"I reckon we should tie him to that tree down by the river."

"Fine by me. Are we going to kill him or let him bleed out?"

"I'll check his pulse and vital signs before I make that decision. You did well back there. I'm proud of you."

"You didn't think I had it in me, did you?"

"Any doubts I might have had, you crushed them."

THEY ARRIVED at the location and opened the van doors to find Parry stirring. He stared at them, his eyes pleading with them to let him go.

After checking the area was clear, they removed him from the van. The driver held Parry's upper body, and his accomplice secured his legs in a tight grip. Together, they walked twenty feet to a large oak tree. The accomplice dropped Parry's legs on the ground and ran back to the van to collect the holdall.

The driver propped Parry up against the trunk. He was muttering something indecipherable behind the tape. As the location was remote and there was no one around, he removed the tape to see what Parry had to say for himself.

"The pain, it's excruciating. You need to take me to the hospital. I'll die otherwise."

"By Jove, I think it's sunk in, at last. That's the intention. It has been all along. We couldn't give a flying fuck about your money. Correction, dirty money. We just wanted to show you how much your devious actions have destroyed our village and wrecked people's lives."

"What the hell are you talking about? What village?"

His accomplice arrived and placed the holdall beside the driver. "Think about it. You're on the parish council there."

"You mean Wilton?"

"You know full well which village I'm talking about. You've let us down, taken us for a bunch of fools. Lied to the residents over and over, and now you're going to suffer the consequences of your deceit."

"I don't know what you're talking about. I have a right to know before you—"

"Kill you? You make me sick. I've already shown you the evidence. People like you need to know that the decisions you make have ramifications on dozens of people, not that you care. You don't even live in the village, so why should you be bothered about it, right?"

"You're wrong. I care deeply about Wilton. I grew up there as a child. Anyone living in the village will tell you that. I'm sorry if you believe I've let you down. Give me the opportunity to put things right. Yes, I can do that, given the chance."

"You've had your chance. You took the wrong path. Decided you would be better off taking backhanders from the likes of Windsor rather than speaking out against him. Threaten you, did he? Like he's threatened some of our neighbours?"

"No, not at all. I don't know what you're talking about. I have done nothing underhand, I promise you."

"You're still insisting that the camera lied, are you? Oh, and, by the way, I've been busy at work, or should I say, in my lunch hour. I've uploaded the footage of you accepting a bribe from Windsor to several sites. You should see the reaction I've had from folks in the area. Wait, I'll show them to you before we finish you. Just to let you know how much you're hated in this community." He removed his mobile from his pocket and scrolled through the dozens of comments the clips had received.

'I've always known he was dodgy, corrupt bastard.'

'He should be kicked off the council. Mind you, I bet they're all taking backhanders down there.'

'What a tosser! How dare he let down our community like that? The bloke deserves everything that is coming his way after this revelation.'

"And that's just a few of them. Want to hear more, do you? I can oblige, if that's what you want."

"I don't. You've ruined my career. You might as well finish me now."

The driver leaned down and sneered, "We don't need your permission to do anything, you hear me?"

"Can we get this over with?" his partner urged. "The weather is going to turn on us."

The driver removed a length of rope from the holdall and wrapped it around Parry's middle and the tree a couple of times. He tested it to ensure it was tight, not caring if Parry thought it was too restrictive. Then he removed a knife from the bag and handed it to his accomplice.

"There you are. You said you wanted to do the deed."

Before taking the knife, his partner removed their mask.

Parry gasped and whispered, "You? How could you do this to me?"

"What are you doing? Why let him see who you are?"

"Don't be ridiculous. Take your mask off. What does it matter if he sees us or not?"

After a moment's hesitation, the driver also removed his mask. "Surprise!"

"Jesus, of all the people, I never thought it would be you two. Why? I've bent over backwards to help you over the last ten years, and this is how you repay me."

"Bollocks have you. You've helped us out with a few minor issues, but when it came to the crunch of fighting the big boys, you've always proved you haven't got the courage. Well, this is our way of dealing with cowards." He faced his partner and said, "Right, it's over to you. Make it quick. We should get out of here."

Parry shook his head. "No, don't do this. Tell me what I can do to make it right."

"It's too late for that, far too late. The damage has been done, and there's no undoing it. Stop whining and accept your fate like a man, not a mouse." The knife plunged into his stomach, just below the rope, followed by a second strike higher up, where the tip of the blade hit a rib.

Parry cried out for help. Of course, no one came to his rescue. "You can't leave me here. I'll die, all alone, where no one will find me. How will you be able to live with yourselves? I'm telling you, you won't be able to. I know that deep down you're good people and that this has all been a complete misunderstanding. Something we can sort out between us."

The blade was then thrust at his chest. The shock registered on Parry's face as the realisation dawned that there was no way he was going to get out of this situation alive. "Don't do it. You've had your revenge, your fun. If you take me to the hospital now, this will remain between us. I promise I won't go to the police."

They both laughed.

The driver checked Parry's pulse; it was slowing down. "He'll be gone soon. Let's leave him now. He can bleed out; sit there and reflect on all the dodgy deals he's been involved with over the years. I have nothing further to say to him."

The driver picked up the holdall and tapped his partner on the shoulder. "Come on, let's get out of here. Have a nice life, Parry, what's left of it. The village, no, make that the world, will be better off without you."

"Come back, please. You can't leave me here."

He listened to Parry begging until they reached the van.

"Tosser, we showed him we're not to be messed with, didn't we?" the accomplice said.

The driver chuckled. "We did." He strained an ear; Parry's shouting had ceased. He was tempted to run back and check on him, but decided against the idea as quickly as it had surfaced. "He's gone. We should get a move on."

"Good. He made my skin crawl. I think we made the right decision, showing him who we were."

"Let's hope he doesn't come back to haunt us."

CHAPTER 8

Sara hit the siren and then cruised through the town to get to the scene. Lorraine had requested they join her on the outskirts of the city, down by the River Wye. Sara drew the car to a halt beside a SOCO van, and they slipped on their protective suits. "I can hear voices over to the left. We'll head over that way."

Lorraine was issuing orders to the techs.

Sara's gaze was drawn to the man tied to the tree. "Shit."

Lorraine rushed to be by her side. "What's wrong? Do you know him?"

"Yes, he's Councillor Alex Parry."

"Bugger, of course he is. I had a feeling I'd seen him before."

"Who found him?" Sara asked.

"A jogger, over to the right. He's pretty shaken up and eager to get home. He needs to be at work."

"I'll have a quick word with him and send him on his way. I'll be back in a sec." Sara approached the man who was talking to a female uniformed officer. "Hello, sir. Forgive me,

I won't come any closer in case I contaminate my suit. Can you tell me if you saw anyone else in the area when you found the victim?"

"No, there was no one else around. Did I do the right thing, you know, calling you?"

"Yes, it's always wise to ring nine-nine-nine in cases such as this. I won't keep you waiting much longer. Can you give the officer your details, and someone will be in touch to take a statement from you in the next few days?"

"Thanks. I've got an important meeting to attend at eleven with my area manager. He's got the patience of a gnat."

"I understand. I'm so sorry you had to witness this scene today. Thank you for calling it in."

"No problem. Took the wind out of me when I first saw him."

"I'm sure. We'll be in touch soon." Sara returned to the crime scene. "We need to get the ball rolling on this one quickly. I didn't ask the witness if he recognised him or not, but if he did, then I think he'll get on to the press right away."

"Thanks for the heads-up. We'll ensure the cordon is set up quickly. Can you ask for extra bodies to join us, just in case?"

"I'll do it," Carla volunteered and stepped away from them.

"Jesus, what the fuck is going on in Hereford at the moment? No sign of a vehicle around, so he was obviously dumped here," Sara said, more to herself than to Lorraine.

"Great observations. Do you want me to run through the injuries he's received?"

"Sorry, go on, surprise me. He's a bloody mess from where I'm standing."

"Someone tortured him and either killed him before they departed or left him here to die a very painful death."

"No tape over his mouth, so they must have been confident no one would hear him. What's the time of death? Or can't you give me that yet?"

"Whoa, lady, calm down. We've not long arrived ourselves; I was organising my team, in case you missed it. And for your information, I believe there was tape over his mouth at one point."

"All right, sorry, I'm trying to speed things up a bit because I know I'm going to get bombarded with questions from the media soon."

"I don't doubt that, but there are certain things that can't be rushed."

Sara closed her eyes and inhaled a deep breath. "Shit, this is not what I bloody need right now."

"What's going on, Sara? I don't mind telling you I think you're acting weirdly. Why?"

"Because I happen to know Councillor Parry here was a member of the Wilton Parish Council, just like the other two victims."

"Shit, shit, shit," Lorraine replied.

They both stared at the victim.

Carla joined them. "They're sending more men out here. Am I interrupting something here?" Her gaze shifted swiftly between Lorraine and Sara.

"We need to leave this with you, Lorraine, and get on the road again. Sorry to run out on you," Sara said and raced towards the car before Lorraine could reply.

"Wait for me, Sara. Slow down, we need to strip off our protective gear first," Carla shouted after her.

"Damn. I'm on it. Get a move on, Carla."

"Where are we going?"

They supported each other and removed the suits.

"We've got to get to his house. Tell his wife, if he has one, before the bloody press shows up there."

"I hear you, but you've got to promise me you won't drive like a maniac to get there."

"I promise. Now hurry and get in the car."

CARLA RANG the station on the way back to the car and got Parry's home address from Jill.

Sara drew up outside the large detached thatched cottage. "Nice pad. Not surprised, given his occupation."

"Let's hope the wife is at home." Carla pointed at a downstairs window. "I think we're in luck."

They walked up the path.

Before Sara could ring the bell, a woman in her early fifties opened the door. "I thought you were coming to me. Who are you?"

Sara and Carla showed their warrant cards.

"Would it be all right if we came in and spoke with you, Mrs Parry?" Sara asked.

"If you must. What's this about?"

Sara didn't answer until they were safely inside the house. "Maybe it would be better if we took a seat."

"Oh God, now you're worrying me. Has something happened to my mother? Has she had a fall again in the home?"

"Please, is there somewhere we can sit down?"

"Through here. The lounge is a mess because I'm doing some art and crafts in there for a function I have coming up at the community centre."

"Anywhere will do."

She showed them into the kitchen and invited them to sit at the dining table. "You didn't answer me. Is this to do with my mother?"

"No. It's about your husband."

Her brow furrowed, and she tutted. "What's he been up to now?"

"It is with regret that I have to tell you his body was discovered this morning."

"His body? I don't believe it. Is this some kind of prank?"

Sara shook her head. "No, not at all. I'm sorry if the news has come as a shock to you, but can you tell us when you last saw your husband alive?"

Mrs Parry seemed stunned but far from upset, which puzzled Sara.

"Two days ago. I stayed at a friend's house for a couple of nights."

Intrigued by the statement, Sara asked, "May I ask why?"

"Because Alex and I have been having a few problems lately, and I needed to get away from him. Are you sure he's dead? That it was him?"

"Pretty sure, although we will need you to positively ID him at the mortuary."

"Shit! Do I really have to?"

"I appreciate you weren't on the best of terms."

"That's an understatement. I asked him for a divorce. He was cheating on me, and I found out about it. It's not the first time the bastard has done it, either."

"I'm sorry to hear that. Do you know who he was seeing?"

"His damn secretary. All low-cut tops and no knickers. He's denied it for months, but I ended up hiring a private investigator, and he soon produced the evidence. I tackled him about it a couple of days ago. He finally admitted he was having an affair and pleaded with me to forgive him. Nope, wasn't going to happen. Sick to death of forgiving and forgetting."

"Do you know how long the affair had been going on?"

"No, and I don't care. I hated the man, and before you ask,

no, not enough to want him dead or even to consider killing him. Can I ask where he died and how?" Her hands clenched together in her lap. She released one of them to tuck a clump of stray hair behind her ear.

"We believe he was probably abducted and tortured before the killer or killers finally ended his life. Do you know much about his secretary?"

"Her name is Kimberley Manning. She's single, at least I think she is, unless he lied to me; I wouldn't have put it past him. I've caught him lying several times during our marriage. That always left a sour taste in my mouth. He was a conniving, deceitful man. That's not me speaking ill of the dead, either."

Sara's eyes narrowed as she ran through the evidence they had already collated during the investigation. "He was a councillor. Are you talking inappropriate use of council funds, that type of thing?"

"Feel free to call it that. I warned him time and time again that one of these days he'd get caught out."

"Has anyone made any threats towards him?"

"Plenty of times, although I can't think of anything specific that's happened recently." Her gaze dropped to the floor.

Sara couldn't help wondering if the anger was giving way to other emotions. "Are you all right? Do you want to stop for a moment?"

"I'm fine. I just need to figure out what to do next. I've never had to deal with anything like this before. Do you know what the procedure is?"

"As I stated previously, you'll have to first identify the body. I wouldn't worry about anything else for a few days. His body probably won't be released right away. Maybe a friend or another family member will advise you."

"Yes, I'll ask Bella. She lost her mother a little while ago. I always thought it would be my mum I'd be sorting out a funeral for next, not my husband."

"Is your mother ill?"

"Yes, she has dementia and is living in a home now. I tried to care for her, to keep her at home, but it was an impossible task. Actually, Alex used that as an excuse, for seeking comfort elsewhere, in the arms of his tart of a secretary. How dare he?"

"That was uncalled for. Sorry you had to go through that. Sometimes guilty parties make sure they blame others for their own weaknesses. Do you know where Kimberley Manning lives?"

"Not too far from here, no idea of her actual address. I think he used to give her a lift now and again. God, I don't even want to think about what they got up to on the way home in that car."

"It would be better not to go there."

Mrs Parry bolted upright as a thought struck her. "Wait, yes, I have it somewhere. The PI gave me a report of what Alex was up to. Let me see if I can find it for you."

"That would be great, if you wouldn't mind sharing it with us."

She left the room, and Carla leaned in to say, "She didn't seem that upset about his death."

"I don't blame her, do you? I think her emotions are in turmoil if she hated the man for having an affair and they were on the verge of going through a divorce." Sara's mobile rang, and she broke off what she was saying to answer it. "Hi, Jill. What have you got for us?"

"Sorry to interrupt, boss, but I thought you should know about this right away. A video was posted on a website yesterday. It clearly shows Councillor Alex Parry receiving a wad of money from the farmer out at Wilton."

"He what? Crap, okay. Can you tell how many hits it has had?"

"Thousands so far. I'm sure that will increase during the course of the day, once the news about his death gets out."

"Shit. It could jeopardise our investigation. Okay, we're interviewing the wife right now." Sara lowered her voice and added, "They were on the verge of seeking a divorce, the reason being, he's been having a fling with his secretary, Kimberley Manning. The wife is trying to find us her address now. While you're on the phone, can you see what you can find out about the woman for me?"

"I'll get on it now. Do you want me to send you the link to the video so you can see it for yourself?"

"Yes, fire it over to me. I'll view it before she returns. Well done for finding it, Jill."

"It's on the way, boss. My pleasure."

"Keep your eye open for anything else doing the rounds. The killer might post how or why they killed him. Also, can you see if the tech guys can tell us who posted the video?"

"I've already actioned that, boss. I know how long the process can take. I've got an alert out there, so if anything else shows up, we should hear about it right away."

"Excellent news. Thanks, Jill." Sara ended the call and just had enough time to view the footage before Mrs Parry entered the room.

"Sorry to be so long. I couldn't remember where I'd hidden it. I didn't want Alex getting his hands on it." She frowned and handed Sara the address. "Has something else happened?"

Sara held her phone up. "Press play to view the video."

Mrs Parry sat on the end of the sofa and watched the footage. "Oh my, caught in the act, wasn't he? Does this mean someone was stalking him? Ready to pounce and punish him after seeing this?"

"Possibly. My team is investigating who posted the video. Did you know your husband was in the habit of taking back-handers?"

"Like I said, he was a very deceitful man, so I'm not surprised to see the evidence. People get sloppy when they think they're above the law, don't they?"

"You're right, we witness that a lot. How are you holding up?"

"I'll survive. I have my mother's genes; she was a very strong woman in her day. I've never been totally reliant on my husband. I've always kept my independence and worked throughout our marriage."

"What do you do?"

"I'm a creative person. Have my own business selling arts and crafts. I attend quite a few of the local shows. But I also sell a fair bit through my website."

"It's always good for a woman to have an interest or career outside their marriage. It stops us from getting stale, doesn't it?"

"My sentiments exactly. Alex wasn't keen on me starting up the business from home, but I put my foot down to prevent his bullying tactics. He was out at work all day and attended the parish councils most of the time, anyway. I'm not the type to sit around, twiddling my thumbs."

"About that... he was a member of the Wilton Parish Council, wasn't he?"

"That's right. I told him he should give it up after we moved, but he was having none of it." Her eyes narrowed. "Wait a minute, there have been two deaths in that village this week. You're not suggesting Alex's murder has anything to do with the others, are you?"

"Possibly. It's a line of enquiry that we need to investigate. Did he know Paul Gains and Victoria Holt well?"

"I'm not sure. I suppose he must have done through the

council meetings. I'm not sure if they always saw eye to eye, though. Sometimes he'd come home from a meeting, pulling his hair out when one or two of the other members spoke out against him concerning any points that had been raised. He didn't appreciate that. He thought his experience of being on the county council would add extra weight at the parish council meetings."

"Understandable. Is there anything else you can tell us about your husband? Was he a member of any clubs, perhaps?"

"No, he had enough on his plate—what with his extra-marital affair thrown into the mix. God, I can't believe it has come to this. I know this is an awful thing to say. Please don't hate me for it, but I'm glad he's dead. I've never said that about anyone in my life before." She placed her head in her hands and expelled a couple of large breaths.

Sara reached over and touched her arm. "Can I get you a drink?"

"I'll have one when you leave. Is there anything else you need to know?"

"No, I don't think so. We'll visit his office. Maybe they'll be able to give us an idea of his movements over the last day or so, if you were away."

"Good idea. His floozy is bound to know. It wouldn't surprise me if he had brought her here while I was away. That reminds me, I need to change the sheets, just in case." She shuddered. "The thought of them having sex in my bed."

"We'll leave you to it. I'll give you one of my cards. Should anything else come to mind, don't hesitate to get in touch."

"Thanks, I don't think it will." She showed them to the front door and shook their hands. "Thank you for coming out here to tell me in person."

"Our pleasure. Take care of yourself. It might be an idea

to call on a friend or a family member to come and sit with you for a while."

"I'll be fine, but thanks all the same. Good luck finding who did this to him. I suppose I'd better give his parents a call now. Not something I'm looking forward to doing. We haven't exactly seen eye to eye for years."

"In that case, I think you'll be the one who needs the luck."

She smiled and closed the door.

"That's one of the strangest interviews we've ever had with a next of kin," Carla whispered as they returned to the car.

"I know, bummer. Now we have to tell the secretary and deal with her breaking down on us."

"Presumptuous on your part."

"Is it? Wanna put some money on it?"

"I'd rather not, because you're rarely wrong."

"Correct. Get in the car."

THEY DREW up in the car park opposite the council offices and walked across the road. Sara showed her warrant card to the middle-aged, officious-looking woman sitting behind the reception desk.

"We'd like to see Kimberley Manning, if she's available."

"Oh, I see. Can I ask what this is in connection with?"

"No, it's a private matter. Is she here?"

"Yes, I saw her pop through the inner door to another office only half an hour ago. Let me see if I can track her down for you."

"I'd appreciate it."

They stepped away from the counter so the receptionist could make the call.

"She'll be right down. Give her a couple of minutes."

"Thanks for your help." Sara pointed at the seating area over to the right. "We might as well wait over there."

The lift doors opened, and a young blonde woman rushed out and headed their way. "I'm Kimberley. How can I help you?"

"Is there somewhere private we can speak?"

"Yes, let me see if this office is free." She poked her head around the door to the room just behind her. "It's a bit snug in there."

"I'm sure it will be okay."

Once inside the room, which turned out to be a supply room fitted with Zamba shelving full of reams of paper and packets of notebooks, sitting alongside boxes of envelopes, the woman clasped her hands in front of her. "Have I done something wrong?"

Avoiding the question, Sara said, "We're here to make enquiries about your boss, Alex Parry."

"Oh, what is it you want to know? He hasn't come in to work for a few days, and I've tried to reach him but haven't been able to get hold of him. Is he all right?"

"Sadly not. When was the last time you saw him?"

"The day before yesterday. What's happened to him?" The colour drained from her rosy cheeks, and she rested her hand on the shelf behind for support.

"I'm sorry to have to inform you that his body was found this morning, down by the river."

"His… body? Are you telling me he's dead?"

Sara nodded and watched the woman collapse in a heap on the floor. "No, he can't be. He just can't be."

"Are you all right? Do you need a hand getting up?"

"No, I think I'd better stay here. I don't think my legs will support me."

"Whatever is best for you. When was the last time you had any contact with him?"

"I told you, I haven't seen him for a few days. I've been going frantic."

"Because you couldn't get hold of him?"

Kimberley sniffled and nodded. "Yes."

"Did you try calling his wife?"

"No. I rang his mobile but didn't get a response. I never dreamed that something bad might have happened to him. He gave me a lift home the night before last. That was the final time — the last time I saw him."

"And how did he seem to you?"

"Fine, his usual chirpy self. Are you telling me that someone has killed him? Or did his car go off the road and it's only just been discovered?"

"No, the former. We believe he was murdered."

Kimberley's mouth gaped open for a moment and then closed, and the tears flowed freely.

Sara glanced Carla's way, and her partner rolled her eyes.

Sara's patience was diminishing fast. "Please, Miss Manning, why don't you get to your feet now?"

"I can't. My legs won't hold me up."

"Sergeant, would you mind getting a chair from the reception area? If they're not bolted down."

Carla left the room and returned with a lightweight orange plastic chair. There was just enough room to place it beside Kimberley, who clawed at it and used it to pull herself up onto her feet.

"Thank you. Have you told her?"

"If you're referring to Mrs Parry, yes, we've just come from the family home."

"And how did she take it?" Her tone was abrupt, snarky even.

"As one would expect. She told us you two were having an affair. Were you aware that she knew?"

"Yes, Alex told me she'd employed a PI to spy on us."

"Spy on you? She had a right to know if her husband was cheating on her, didn't she?"

Kimberley sniffled again. "I suppose so. He was going to leave her. He told me he wanted to share the rest of his life with me. He was waiting for the right time to tell her."

"Not that old chestnut," Sara replied and resisted the temptation to laugh.

"We loved each other. I believed him," Kimberley shouted defensively.

"Did he tell you this before or after his wife suspected the affair?"

"I don't know. Why are you asking me all these questions? You should be out there, searching for his killer, not wasting time here, asking inane questions."

"Hardly inane questions, Miss Manning. We're conducting a murder inquiry, we have procedures to follow. Do you have a boyfriend or husband?"

"No, I've been single for years."

"And how long have you been sleeping? Forgive me, seeing your boss romantically?"

"For the last five months. Up until then, we were good friends and work colleagues. I can't believe he's gone. Do you know who killed him?"

"We were hoping you might help us out there."

"What are you talking about? Am I a suspect? How could you even believe that of me? I would never hurt Alex."

"What about his colleagues? Has he fallen out with anyone lately?"

"He was always falling out with people—in his mind, he was always right."

"So we've been told. What about any threats?"

"What about them? Did he have any? Is that what you're asking?"

"Yes."

"No, or if he did, he didn't tell me. You think his death is work related? What if the killer comes after me?"

Sara inclined her head. "Why would they do that?"

"How would I know? What are you accusing me of? Are you insinuating that I'm behind his murder? You couldn't be more wrong. I loved that man, thought the bloody world of him, and here you are…" She broke down again.

"I'm not insinuating anything of the sort, simply asking you pertinent questions that might lead us to the person who killed your boss, your lover, call him what you like," Sara raised her voice; she could see Carla turn to face her but refused to look her way. "I'm sorry, that was harsh. It's been a tough week. This is the third murder we've had to deal with."

"It's okay. I guess it's logical for you to question me, me being his mistress. I've brought it on myself. The murders, are they all connected? If not, how can you possibly be working on three different investigations at the same time? I know the police budget in this area has been cut. He was privy to the information. I used to hear about it all the time, when he was alive…"

"Yes, we believe the deaths might be connected. Has Alex ever confided in you? Perhaps he told you he had suspicions that someone was following him."

"No, nothing along those lines at all. He didn't even know the PI was following us. That came as a shock to both of us when the truth came out."

"While we're on the premises, will you give us permission to search his office?"

"Don't you need a search warrant for that? I mean, we're talking about a government department here, and it'll be my head on the chopping block if I give you access and you see something you shouldn't do in there. Sorry, I'm chuntering on, it's the shock."

"Don't worry, we have other people we need to visit,

anyway. If it's going to put you in an awkward position, we'll go down the proper route and obtain a search warrant. Are you going to be all right?"

"I think so. I'm sorry if I couldn't supply the answers you needed. Do you have a card? I might think of something important after you leave."

"Yes." Sara dipped her hand into her pocket and handed the young woman a card.

Kimberley rose from her seat. Her legs were still a little wobbly until she reached the reception area.

"Thanks for talking with us."

"Can I go now?"

"Yes, you're free to go. Oh, no, wait. Who can help us get footage from the CCTV cameras on the premises?"

"We have a security guard here, at least I think we do. Rachel at reception can give you the details. May I ask why?"

"I'm simply ensuring I have all the evidence I need to investigate the case thoroughly. Thanks, leave it with us, we'll sort it."

"As you wish." With that, Kimberley trotted off on her four-inch stiletto heels and hopped into the lift once more.

Rachel watched them warily as they approached her desk.

"Hi, is the security guard on site at present?" Sara asked.

"He's on a break. Can I help?"

"I don't think so. Where are we likely to find him?"

"I'll call him, ask him if he's willing to see you. He's entitled to his break, like everyone else is around here."

"Ask the question. If he refuses to see us, then we'll sit over here and wait for him."

"I'll do my best for you." She made the call, and within a few seconds, a man in his fifties came to a screeching halt before the receptionist could replace her phone in the base station.

"You rang," he gasped, slightly out of breath.

"Keith, can you have a word with these two detectives, please?"

"Always keen to help the police. With what?"

"I'm not sure." The phone rang, and she answered it.

Keith smiled and came to a stop in front of Sara.

"Thanks for agreeing to see us," she said. "Sorry if we're disturbing your break."

"It's okay. I'm used to drinking cold coffee. How can I help?"

"We're keen to see the footage from two nights ago, around the time Councillor Parry left the premises."

He rubbed his hands together and grinned. "I love playing detective. Come this way, ladies. Don't get too excited, my office is pretty cramped, but I take pride in keeping it tidy."

"Don't mind us. Hopefully, we won't keep you too long."

Once they'd reached the small room, Sara wouldn't classify it as an office. Keith removed a disc case from the shelf and inserted the disc into the machine. "He usually leaves between six and six-fifteen, so I'll whizz past everyone else leaving, if that's all right? I can always come back."

"Sounds good to me."

Sara kept a close eye on the time on the screen and asked him to stop when it got to five-fifty. "Can you stop it there?"

"It's too early for him," Keith replied.

"But it might give us the information we're after."

"I'm not with you," he replied, puzzled. "Are you going to tell me what this is all about?"

"Mr Parry went missing around this time. He's since been found murdered."

"Well, stone the bloody crows. I wasn't expecting you to say that. Jeez... shocked me to the core, that has, good and proper, like."

"So, we need to examine the car park opposite, if possible, to see if there was a vehicle waiting for him."

"I'm with you. I can tell you if there are any strange vehicles over the road or not." He kept a close eye on the video and pointed to a van as it came into view. "That's a new one. Let's see if he pays for a ticket."

The driver of the van parked towards the rear of the car park and remained in his vehicle.

"Can you get the registration number for me?"

"I would, if there was one on the van. That's suspicious in itself, isn't it?"

Sara nodded her agreement. "Any signage on the side?"

"I can see something," Carla said and took a step closer. "Far too small and fuzzy for my eyesight."

"I've got no chance of reading it then. Your eyesight is A1 compared to mine. Can you fast forward? That has to be the vehicle we're after."

The image sped up, and Keith stopped it again when Alex and Kimberley left the building together and walked across the road to his vehicle.

"That's his secretary. I shouldn't say this, but the rumour mill is in full swing about those two—or it was."

"We're aware they were having an affair."

"Oh right, I wasn't sure if you'd know or not."

The couple entered Parry's vehicle and immediately left the car park with the van they'd already spotted in tow, close behind them.

"Looks like we were right," Carla said. She stepped closer to the screen. "Bugger, they've plastered something over the side of the van to cover up the signage."

"I wouldn't expect anything less from the killers, would you?"

"I suppose not."

"Keith, can we have a copy of the disc? Would you mind?"

"Not at all. It'd be my pleasure." He removed another disc from its case, slotted it in the other side of the machine, and pressed the Record button. "Can I say something? You might think I'm speaking out of turn if I do."

"You're free to say anything."

"I've never liked that bloke, smarmy shit most of the time. He always looked down his nose at people, as if they were beneath him. I know I'm just a security guard, but everyone else treats me like a colleague. Not him. She's all right, but she should have known better. They thought they were being discreet, but everyone and their dog knew they were having an affair. Disgusting way to behave for a councillor, if you ask me, and him, a married man."

"Do you think anyone in this building thought badly enough about Parry to want to kill him?"

"I doubt it. We're decent folks around here. However, I'm not surprised someone had it in for him. It wasn't a case of if, but when, he was going to upset someone badly enough that they'd want to kill him. Don't get me wrong, I'm sorry that he's dead, just not surprised, that's all."

"I can understand that. You've been really helpful. We'll get this disc off to the lab, see what forensics can pick up for us."

"Always glad to help the police. I wanted to join up years ago but failed the medical, dodgy ticker at the time. I've since had a pacemaker and a double valve operation to put that right. Still, you don't want to hear me going on about what might have been, not when you have an important case to solve."

"Thanks. If you hear any gossip relevant to the investigation about the councillor, will you give me a call?" Sara handed him one of her cards.

"I'll be sure to do that. I hope you find the person responsible, soon."

"So do we. Thanks again for all your help."

They left the council office and made their way back to the car.

"I'll stop off at the lab en route, see what they can come up with for us," Sara said.

"Where do we go from here?"

"Apart from the usual, checking the cameras throughout the city relating to the van, I think we should head back to Wilton and have a chat with the only other member of the parish council whom we haven't spoken to yet."

Carla removed her notebook from her pocket and flipped it open. "Gordon Abbott. Want me to find an address for him?"

"Great stuff. Check online to see if there are any articles relating to either him or the Parish Council over the last six months. While you're at it you might as well check. We've got half an hour to kill."

"I can take a hint. Instead of me admiring the views, you'd rather get me working."

"You catch on quickly, sometimes."

"You can go off some people," Carla mumbled.

Sara laughed. "Truth be told, I'm surprised our friendship has lasted as long as it has."

Carla muttered something indecipherable and began scrolling through her phone.

The journey gave Sara the chance to review the different angles of the investigation in her mind. The connection must be with the parish council, but why? What about the farmer we witnessed handing over the money in that video? We need to speak with him after we've visited Abbott. And then there's the Environmental Health angle as well. After what happened with the previous corrupt officer, would they really risk throwing themselves into the spotlight again so soon?

"Are you with me?" Carla nudged her elbow.

"Sorry, I had drifted off."

"Thinking about the funeral?"

Sara shook her head. "Far from it. I was going over the possibilities of who the killer might be and what their motive is."

"It's a toughie. I've found a few articles of interest about Abbott."

"Don't keep me in suspense, spill."

"Most of it is good. He seems to do more for the community than the others, apart from Paul Gains, of course. I'd say he is trying to make a difference to a specific group in the village, the pensioners. Always fighting for their rights and has been known to hold a fundraiser here and there for a specific person's needs since Covid struck."

"He sounds a better person than Parry, in that respect, who clearly had his own agenda at the forefront of his mind at all times."

"You're not wrong." Carla shuddered. "I wouldn't say this to anyone else, only because we're alone, but he gave me the willies. I don't know how anyone in their right mind would find him attractive."

"Maybe he had a magic willy that... nope, I'm not going there, and I need to shake that image from my mind ASAP. It's your fault for planting it there in the first place."

"There's a surprise. I knew it would be my fault. Anyway, I've managed to locate Abbott's address, it was one of the houses we knocked on the other day."

"And?"

"There was no one home."

Sara scratched the back of her head. "Hmm... that could be deemed a suspicious coincidence, couldn't it?"

"Possibly. We could head back to the village and ask the

neighbours if they know where he is or if they have a phone number for him."

"You read my mind. Right, the lab first, and then we'll haul our arses back to Wilton again. We'll know that place like the back of our hands soon."

"You're not wrong. I can't help but sense we're letting the residents down, though. We should have caught the killers by now."

"Stop being so hard on yourself. Don't forget, we're investigating three different murders and all that entails. The countless hours of speaking to the neighbours, the next of kins et cetera. I think we're getting somewhere now. We have to be, don't we?"

"Let's hope so."

THE TECH at the lab promised he would get the results back to Sara by the end of his working day, which was the same time she generally clocked off at around six. Whether that would be the case today was anyone's guess.

Sara drove out to Wilton and drew up outside a detached property set back from the road a little. There was a large driveway, a patch of square lawn and flower borders on three sides of it. A white BMW was parked on the drive.

"They're away at the moment," a man shouted over the fence from next door.

Sara crossed the lawn to speak with him. "Any idea when they're going to be back?"

"At the weekend, I think. You're the police, aren't you?"

Sara flashed her ID. "That's right. I don't suppose you have a phone number for him, do you?"

"As it happens, yes, I do." He went inside the house and came out with a slip of paper. "I haven't been in touch with him since he left. There was some kind of family emergency up north. Manchester, I believe."

"Thanks. You've been very helpful." Sara turned her back on the neighbour and rang the number. "Mr Abbott?"

"That's right. I'm driving. Can you make this quick?"

"I'm DI Sara Ramsey of the West Mercia Police. Can you pull over and speak with me for a moment?"

"Goodness, yes, we're in luck. There's a lay-by up ahead." Several moments later, he sighed. "Right, I've stopped the vehicle. What can I do for you? Is this about what's happening in the village?"

"You're aware of what's been going on, sir?"

"We have a TV in our campervan. We're keeping up with the news. Actually, we decided this morning to return home. My father was admitted to the hospital. He's recovering now, so we're able to leave him. Can you tell me what you know to date?"

Sara gave him a brief rundown of the events that had happened since the beginning of the week.

"I knew Paul had been killed. I held the public meeting the following day, then Mum rang and asked us to be with her. We packed up and set off the next morning. Goodness me, my wife and I have been struggling to get our heads around it ever since."

"I know. It's hard to understand. We're doing our very best to make sense of things. Something you won't be aware of is that Alex Parry was also found murdered this morning."

Silence filled the line.

"Mr Abbott, are you still there?"

"Yes, bloody hell. Does this mean I could be the killer's next target?"

"Without wishing to cause you concern, we believe that's a distinct possibility. How far away are you?"

"About an hour. Why?"

"Is there somewhere local you can stay? With a friend or a family member, perhaps?"

"I'm sure we can sort something out. Should we come and see you at the station?"

"When you get settled, I think it would be better if I came out to visit you. I'm in and out all day long."

"Yes, maybe that would be for the best. I'll get June to make some calls and get back to you with the decision we make."

"I'll look forward to hearing from you soon."

He ended the call after a mumbled farewell. Sara thanked the neighbour, who was lingering on the other side of his garden, and handed the sheet of paper back to him.

"Thanks for your help."

"I couldn't help overhearing. Are Gordon and June on their way back?"

"They are, but they're going to find somewhere else to stay as a temporary measure."

"I don't blame them. What about the other residents in the village? Are we safe?"

Sara shrugged. "I hope so. Maybe it would be better if you kept vigilant for now."

"What, until you find the killers?"

"If you're concerned, then yes, perhaps you should consider it."

"Sod that. I love pottering around in my garden when the weather is dry. The winter is long enough as it is."

"That's up to you, sir. Thanks again for your help."

He grunted and turned his back on her.

Sara returned to the car and brought Carla up to date on what Abbott had to say.

"That makes sense," Carla said, "but how is it going to help us find the killer?"

"What are you suggesting? That we should have used Abbott as bait in some kind of trap?"

Carla grinned. "I would."

"Heartless bitch."

Her partner grinned again. "That's me. No, in all seriousness, maybe we should do something along those lines, force the killers to slip up."

"Let's try to be patient. We've got some evidence that has come our way recently. We're dependent on the lab and the phone tech people to come up trumps for us."

"And what should we do in the meantime?"

"Ask me another, preferably one that I can answer."

CHAPTER 9

⌘

A few hours later, the killers were sitting at home, discussing what their next move should be. The hits on the website were close to a hundred thousand now.

"Who knew something like this would be popular? I'm regretting not filming his torture now and throwing that out there as well."

"It's better not to chance our luck too much. It's a shame we have to wait for a while to complete our mission."

At that, the driver glanced up and saw a campervan pass the window. "What the fuck? We might be in luck here. Come on, get your shoes on."

"What are you talking about?"

"I think Abbott has just got back from his trip. We should get out there and see what he's up to."

"In broad daylight, are you crazy?"

The driver paused to contemplate their next move. "Okay, you're right. I still need to know what's going on. We won't bother with the van. We'll take your car instead."

"Do we have to?"

"Stop whining. Like I said, get your shoes on."

He waited impatiently by the front door. His associate took an eternity to get ready. "Get a move on."

"All right, I'm ready now."

They raced out of the house and stood by the Vauxhall Corsa parked on the driveway. He asked for the keys and jumped in, hitting his legs on the steering wheel until he moved the seat back.

"Every damn time!"

His accomplice laughed. "You're supposed to learn from your mistakes."

"Leave it." He drove to the other end of the village, past Abbott's house.

The campervan was parked on the road instead of its usual place on the drive. June Abbott was in the front seat.

"Shit, we can't make a move, not with her watching us."

"I'm glad she's here. We're not prepared, all our gear is in the back of the van. You need to calm down and think straight, we've come too far for you to screw things up now."

"Don't worry, I won't screw it up. I'm going to pull in and keep an eye on them."

They watched Abbott leave the house with his laptop and an overnight bag, which he placed in the side door of the campervan. Then he jumped behind the steering wheel and drove off.

"He's coming past us; he's going to recognise our car. I'm sure he will."

"Just pretend we're having a conversation. We'll let him get up the road a bit and then follow him. I'm intrigued to see where he's going."

"Might be off on their holidays now, and perhaps they stopped off to collect some more clothes on the way."

"Logical, I guess. We'll see what they're up to soon enough." He glanced down at the dashboard and cursed under his breath. "We're short of petrol. What have I told you about keeping it topped up in case of emergencies? We live out in the country."

"Not my fault. You used it last week. I haven't driven it since then, so piss off and stop blaming me for your cockups."

He mumbled an apology and spotted the campervan making a right turn up ahead of them. "Let's hope he's staying local. Maybe the police have suggested it might be too risky for them to return home."

"You're probably right."

They ended up driving ten miles away, out near Kenchester. The driver drew up past the entrance to a farm and ran back to spy on the couple. The Abbotts crossed the courtyard to what appeared to be an annexe to the right, next to the farmhouse, which seemed empty at first glance until he spotted a woman at the window waving at the Abbotts. She came to the door to greet them. They hugged, and then the woman dipped back inside the farmhouse. She returned, dangling a key that she handed to June.

He'd seen enough; he ran back to the car. "Shit, this isn't going our way. They're staying in an annexe with the farmhouse right next to them."

"Bloody hell. How are we going to get to him?"

"Shh... I'm thinking."

"What about their dog? They usually take that with them."

"I heard a dog barking in the background. I thought it belonged to the farmer, though. All is not lost then. We'll sit tight for a few minutes."

They didn't have to wait long before Gordon Abbott appeared at the entrance to the farm with a Yorkshire terrier on a retractable leash. He looked left and right, then crossed the road and headed towards the woodland path opposite the farm.

The driver rubbed his hands with glee. "This is our chance. Are you ready?"

"We can't. We haven't got any masks or equipment with us."

He circled his finger in front of his face. "Bothered? Not. Come on, let's shake a leg and get after him, or try to get ahead of him."

"You're nuts. I don't think I can do this."

"Stay here then. It's not the first time I've had to pick up the slack."

"But we're partners."

"Then act like it and get your arse in gear. Otherwise, he's going to get away from us."

The driver bolted out of the car and ran across the road. His accomplice did their best to keep up with him; he refused to check their progress, not caring either way. He knew he had to take this chance to get hold of Abbott, not knowing when the next opportunity would come their way.

A snap sounded ahead of him.

"Come on, Mickey, get the stick." The dog yapped excitedly, but when Abbott threw the stick, the dog stood its ground and looked up at his master. "Bloody useless. Unless there are treats and cuddles involved, there's no point in having you around, is there?"

The dog barked and leapt on the spot a few times. Abbott moved further through the woodland, his faithful companion dropping into step beside him.

The driver had a feeling it would be now or never to make his move. He upped his pace and before long was within a few feet of Abbott, his target none the wiser about his proximity. He scanned the area around him and picked up a thick branch from the woodland floor. One swipe, and Abbott tumbled to the ground. Mickey barked incessantly and tried to bite him as he reached for Abbott and dragged him behind a thick trunk. He set the dog free and shooed him away.

"Go on, bugger off back to Mummy."

The dog hesitated, obviously confused. The driver clapped his hands together loudly, scaring the mutt. It ran off towards the main road.

Crap, why didn't you run off in the other direction? Your father was right. You're a useless piece of shit.

He placed his hands under Abbott's arms and dragged him along the path, back to the car. His partner was waiting at the entrance to the woodland. "Don't just stand there. Give me a hand."

"What are you doing? What if someone sees us?"

"That's a given if we procrastinate. Shit. Wait here with him. I'll bring the car over."

As he got closer to the vehicle, he heard the Yorkshire terrier yapping outside the annexe.

I should have killed the little shit!

He slipped behind the wheel and drove the car fifty feet up the road and helped his partner toss Abbott's body into the backseat.

Behind them, a woman screamed.

In a panic, the driver shouted, "Get in the car, quickly!"

"Come back here. I'm going to call the police."

SARA RECEIVED the call from a shocked Mrs Abbott moments after her husband was abducted. "Please, Mrs Abbott, I need you to calm down. You're not making any sense."

"I don't want to calm down. They've got him, they've abducted my husband. You have to help me. I know who it is."

"What? You saw your husband being taken?"

"Yes. I wasn't meant to. He took the dog for a walk in the woodland across the road. Mickey found his way home and alerted me. I saw Ben Everard and his mother, Natalie, throwing my husband in the backseat of their car. He was unconscious, or he might have even been dead." She broke down in tears.

Sara covered the mouthpiece and shouted, "They've got Abbott. Get me all the information we have on Natalie and Ben Everard, ASAP." Removing her hand, she spoke to Mrs Abbott again. "Where are you? I'll send some officers to be with you."

"No, I'm fine. I'm with a friend. She's going to look after me. I want you to put all your efforts into finding my husband. Please, please don't let him die."

"Give me your address all the same. I promise, as soon as I hang up, my team and I will get on the road."

"I'm at Sunnyside Farm out at Kenchester."

"I'll still send a car. You shouldn't be alone. If the kidnappers contact you, ring me straight away."

"I will. Please help him before they do the unthinkable to him."

"We're going to do our very best. Take care, lock yourself in over there."

"Already done. My friend Faith has been brilliant. She has a shotgun here."

Sara closed her eyes, imagining the scene. "All right, don't do anything rash. The patrol will be with you soon."

"We won't. Thank you."

Sara ended the call.

"I've found out a few details about the Everards," Jill said. "The son runs a carpet fitting business."

Sara raced across the room towards Jill, who angled her screen. There, In his main photo on Facebook, Ben was standing alongside the van. "Carla, is that the same van?"

Carla joined them and nodded. "It is. I'm ninety-nine percent sure of it."

"Damn, they were on our list to speak to. Why haven't we interviewed them yet?"

"I think that was down to us, or should I say, me," Carla replied. "I knocked on the door, but there was no answer."

Sara rubbed her arm. "Don't go blaming yourself. We need to see what other vehicles they have at their disposal. Mrs Abbott said she saw her husband being bundled onto the backseat but didn't tell me what type of car it was."

"I've got that information here, boss," Marissa shouted. "It's a Vauxhall Corsa."

"Tiny compared to their van. I wonder why they've switched it up. Craig, get that vehicle tracked through the ANPR system. It's not likely to show up soon because they're quite a way out of town, but when they do, we'll throw everything we've got at stopping the bastards."

"On it, boss."

"In the meantime, we need to research the couple and see what we can find out about them. I can't place where their property is located. Is it near the vicarage or the other end of the village?"

"The other end. I believe their property backs onto the farm, which has been causing all the problems over there," Carla informed her.

"Interesting. Okay, I'm going downstairs to have a word with Jeff. I can explain it better in person." Sara shot out of the outer office and ran down the concrete steps to the reception area, only to find the desk sergeant dealing with a member of the public.

"That's right, fill out the form, and I'll go through it with you once you've finished." He gave the older woman a sheet of paper and a pen, and she took a seat to fill it in.

"Can I see you? Do you have someone else to man the desk?"

"Yes, just a minute, ma'am." He poked his head in the room behind the counter, and a young female officer took over the reception desk. He pointed at the interview room they sometimes used for more private conversations if a member of the public requested it. "Shall we go in there?"

"Suits me."

They sat on either side of the desk, and Sara explained the situation to him.

"How many men can you spare me? Bearing in mind, we believe the couple are serial killers and have already claimed three victims."

"How many do you want?"

"As many as possible. Can you send a couple of patrols out that way? Here's the address of where Mrs Abbott is staying. I need to organise protection for her as a priority."

"I'll get this sorted ASAP, ma'am. I'll keep you up to date with how things proceed."

"Cheers, Jeff. Carla and I are going to head out to the Everards' address. Not that I think for one second they're going to take Abbott there, but I need to throw caution to the wind in case they slip up. It's not unheard of for criminals to unravel once they've been seen."

"You're right. I've still got a patrol car monitoring the village. I'll get them to join you at the property."

"No, ask them to meet us at the vicarage instead. The last thing we need is to alert the Everards that we're on the way."

"Leave it with me."

She smiled and patted Jeff on the shoulder. "Let's hope we can find the buggers before they do away with Abbott."

Jeff held up his crossed fingers, and they left the room together.

Sara punched in her code to open the security door and tore up the stairs, her mind stirring up a whirlwind of scenarios. She burst through the door to the outer office and crossed the room towards Craig. "What about using a drone in that area?"

"It makes sense, boss. Do you want me to organise that, see if it's free?"

"Thanks, Craig. Let me know. Have you actioned the ANPR?"

"All done. It's a case of us sitting and waiting for the information to come back to us now."

"That doesn't sit well with me. I'm not really one for sitting around, twiddling my fingers, not when there's a man's life in danger."

"Sorry, I didn't mean to sound so blasé about it, boss."

"You weren't. I was merely stating facts."

Carla came up behind them. "I feel like there's more we could do, but I'm at a loss to know what that is."

"I understand. I've arranged for us to meet up with the officers patrolling the village. Are you ready to go?"

"I'm ready, chomping at the bit."

"Give me two minutes with the team first. I want to make sure we're on the same page before we get on the road."

"I'll nip to the loo before we head off."

THEY MET up in the hallway and raced down the stairs. Sara stopped off at the armoury to sign out a Taser, and then she drove out to the village again, for what seemed like the hundredth time this week. They met up with the patrol car and told the officers to join them, and they arrived at the Everards' home in one vehicle.

"You take the back. Do you have Tasers?"

"Only me," the older male officer replied.

"Be warned, they might be armed. We're after both of

them, the mother and the son, so don't get fooled into thinking the mother has nothing to do with this."

"We won't, ma'am."

Sara and Carla walked up the path to the front door, acting as normally as possible and remaining vigilant.

Carla pointed out the van at the side of the house, the nose of which was jutting out from behind the shed. "They kept it off the road, out of view."

"They're crafty, not to be messed with. Keep alert, just in case."

One of the uniformed officers appeared at the side of the house. "You might want to come and see this, ma'am."

They followed him past the overgrown hedge and into the messiest back garden they'd come across in a while. The fence had been taken down, most likely to bring the van through the side alley and park it at the rear.

The officer led them to the back door. "I tried it. It's unlocked."

"Interesting. It looks like they left in a hurry," Carla said.

"They must have done. They didn't have time to get the van out. I'm wondering if the Abbotts came by the house, possibly to check what post they'd had while they were away or to pick up extra supplies, and the Everards saw them drive past. Their house is at the other end of the village; if they came off the main road, they'd need to pass by this way."

Carla nodded. "And that set the wheels in motion. They probably jumped in the mother's car and followed them out to where the Abbotts were staying."

"Yep. As soon as they got there, Mr Abbott took the dog for a walk. The Everards were more than likely parked up outside the farm, waiting for the opportunity to arise for them to strike."

"I bet they couldn't believe their luck. Shall we have a look inside?"

"Why not? It's an open invitation."

They both snapped on a pair of gloves. Sara noted that the uniformed officers already had theirs in place. Sara opened the back door, and the four of them entered the property and wound their way through the house.

"We're looking for any form of notebook they might have used to plan out the murders. As well as proof of a location where they might have held the third victim, Councillor Parry. My opinion is that they've probably taken Abbott to the same spot. You check upstairs, and we'll carry out the search down here."

The officers ran up the stairs, and Sara led the way into the lounge. There was a small dining table in the bay window with lots of paperwork spread out across the surface.

"Let's see what we can find here." Sara sifted through the sheets of paper. "This all appears to be about the planning application for the farm. It lists a few of the neighbours." She frowned and read out some form of plan that the Everards and others were about to initiate. "Am I reading this right?" She handed the sheet of paper to Carla to get her take on it before she voiced her own opinion.

"It's to do with the public meeting that was held regarding the farm a few days ago."

"That's what I thought. What have we stumbled across here? Are there more than two killers involved, or have these two got it into their heads to take the matter further, without the others being aware of what was going on?"

"I suppose the only way we're going to find out is by questioning the other residents on the list."

Sara growled. "A time suck, if there's nothing to it."

"A necessary exercise, all the same, Sara. We'd be neglecting our duties if we didn't follow the clues."

Sara closed her eyes and sighed. "I know, but a man's life could be in imminent danger."

"But if the others know, they might crumble and tell us where they're keeping him."

"All right, you've convinced me. I'm going to get the rest of the team out here; we can't do this on our own. We should hit them all at the same time, in case they warn each other, or worse still, warn the Everards."

Sara made the call, requesting that Barry, Christine, Marissa and Craig join them, leaving Jill back at the station to man the phones. After which they continued the search of the property until their colleagues showed up.

The two officers who had been rooting around upstairs entered the lounge, looking despondent.

"Sorry, ma'am, we found nothing upstairs. Everything was as it should be, no drawers or wardrobes left open, so no sign of them packing up and leaving in a rush."

"Thanks, okay. We believe we've found what we're looking for here. We're waiting for the rest of the team to join us before we plan our next move. Why don't you go back to your car and keep patrolling the area for us?"

"Yes, ma'am. Good luck."

"Thank you."

FIFTEEN MINUTES LATER, the other team members joined them in the Everards' lounge. Sara went over what they had discovered and asked them to partner up, then allocated each pair with a suspect to interview. "Remember, we're not accusing these people of doing anything unlawful, not at the moment. We have no proof they're involved in the murders; all this is to do with the disruption that is going on at the farm, which in itself is throwing me. But let's deal with the proof we have to hand. We'll meet up outside in half an hour. Craig, before you go, did you sort out the drones?"

"Yes, Dale is on it now, boss. He's got my number. I'll ring you if I hear anything."

"Thanks. Let's hit them hard, folks. We haven't got time to dilly-dally, not with Abbott being abducted."

The team headed out, and Sara and Carla walked across the road to interview Linda Roland. Sara knocked on the door; she had already noticed the woman observing them as they left the Everards' garden. She showed the woman her ID. "May we step inside and speak with you for a moment?"

"Of course." She backed up to the bottom of the stairs. "Come through to the lounge. Does this have anything to do with Natalie and Ben? I saw you over at their house. Are they all right?"

"They're missing at present. Do you know where they might be?"

"Me? Why should I know?"

"We know about the group you've formed with a few of the other neighbours."

"I beg your pardon. What are you insinuating? I have to tell you, I don't care for your tone."

"I'm sorry you feel that way. We have the evidence to hand, proving that a group of you are behind the public meeting that was held in the village hall this week."

"What are you talking about? Behind? We're concerned villagers who believe the parish council is letting us down. That's all our group meetings have been about. How we were going to make the other villagers aware of what was going on down at the farm? Can't you smell it? The stench coming from that place? It's impacting our lives. We were forced to form a group, recognising that it was better to tackle the issues together rather than as individuals."

"There is no denying there is a smell in the village. What was the response from the parish council at the meeting?"

"It wasn't really about them. But the farmer, Ralph Windsor, didn't allow us to have our say on the night. He issued threats via his solicitor, who silenced the crowd and put a dampener on the proceedings."

"And did the parish council members play a role that evening?"

"They did. A couple of them, Councillor Parry and Gordon Abbott. They read out a letter from the farmer, stating that he felt he was being harassed, and another letter from Windsor's solicitor. It turned out to be a farce in the end. Why are you questioning me about this? And why were you over the road at the Everards' house?"

"Do you know where they are?"

"No, should I?"

"Do they have another residence in the area?"

"Not as far as I know. Ben lives with his mother because the property prices have gone through the roof, and he can't afford a house of his own. Is that classed as a criminal offence these days?"

Sara's mobile rang. She removed it from her pocket and saw Craig's name on the screen. "Excuse me while I take this important call."

Linda waved her hand and huffed out a breath. "Don't mind me, I just live here."

Sara left the room and closed the door behind her. "Craig, what have you got for me?"

"News from Dale. He believes he has seen the Corsa at a farm in Canon Bridge.

"Right. Have you finished interviewing your suspect?"

"Yes, they couldn't tell us anything."

"We're in the same situation. Can you contact the others and tell them to wrap things up? We'll meet up outside."

"I'll do that. See you soon, boss."

Sara ended the call, tucked her phone back in her pocket, and returned to the lounge. "Sorry, we have to run. Something important has come up. Thank you for your time, Mrs Roland."

"You mean you sitting here interrogating me when I've done nothing wrong? I have a right to know what's going on with the Everards. Why were you in their house?"

"We're conducting a murder inquiry. Again, thank you for your time. Are you ready, Sergeant?" Sara asked, eager to leave.

Carla flipped her notebook shut and followed Sara out of the house. Mrs Roland shouted something offensive, but Sara didn't have time to reprimand her for her inappropriate behaviour.

They met up with the rest of the team and drove out to Canon Bridge once Craig had supplied them with the exact location.

CHAPTER 10

The convoy of vehicles arrived at the location. Sara contacted all cars and told the members of her team they should approach on foot. They assembled at the start of the lane that led to the farm.

"Do you have any footage from the drone, Craig?"

He removed his phone from his pocket and showed her a clip that Dale had sent him while they were en route to the location.

Seeing the footage, Sara organised the team, giving them specific instructions on how they should proceed. "Is everyone clear on what their role is?"

Her colleagues all nodded. "Carla, you partner up with Barry. Craig, you come with me."

The switch meant Sara wouldn't be the only one with a Taser to hand. She'd teamed up with Craig before and, whilst he was relatively new to the job, he was adept at keeping his cool when the odds were against them.

"Follow my lead, but if I can distract either of them long enough, especially the son, take the shot. Don't wait for me to give you the go ahead, got it?"

"Yes, boss."

"Nervous?"

"You could say that."

"Don't be. We've been in this situation before and succeeded."

"With you by my side, I'm confident we can do this, boss."

"Good man." She high-fived him and then gestured for the others to quietly move forward. "Let's do this," she whispered.

They used the grass verge to creep up to the barn door. It was ajar a couple of inches. Sara cocked her ear and picked up a man pleading for his life—Abbott. He yelled. It was obvious the Everards were torturing him.

Sara nudged Craig and mouthed, "Are you ready? Three, two, one!"

She yanked the door open. Craig went ahead of her, but only by a split second.

"Drop your weapon or I'll fire!" Craig shouted.

The Everards stared at them.

"Please, help me, Inspector," Abbott pleaded.

Ben Everard gripped Abbott around the throat, choking him with his forearm, and his mother stepped away from the two men.

"Don't fire. We'll let him go," Natalie said. "Ben, let him be. Release your hold on him."

"No way. I intend to see this situation to its conclusion. He's going to die."

"You're making a huge mistake, Ben. Listen to your mother, let him go."

"Never."

With her Taser trained on the woman, Sara said, "Natalie, walk towards me slowly and you won't get hurt."

"Okay, please, this has all got out of hand. We didn't mean

to kill anyone. It was the frustration urging us on, wasn't it, Ben?"

"Speak for yourself, Mother. I had no hesitation or second thoughts about venting my anger on the victims, and I'm not finished yet."

A bang sounded behind him, drawing his attention. Sara motioned for Abbott to duck, and Craig fired his Taser. The wires pierced Ben's chest, and he dropped to the floor, fifty thousand volts surging through him.

Sara shouted for the rest of the team to assist them. Carla and Marissa latched on to Natalie's arms and cuffed the distraught woman.

"I'm sorry, I'm sorry. None of this was meant to happen," Natalie said repeatedly.

"Get her out of here," Sara ordered, not prepared to listen to the drivel coming out of the older woman's mouth, not with three murders on the table.

Meanwhile, Craig, along with Barry, had released the wires from Ben's chest. Although he was disoriented, his feisty nature returned rapidly. They hoisted him to his feet and cuffed him before he could find his voice and kick off.

The three men passed Sara. She took a step back, expecting Ben to spit at her, venting his anger. He didn't; instead, he looked her in the eye and shouted, "I regret nothing. They all deserved it. Actually, I have one regret, that you showed up when you did. Five minutes later, and you'd be in charge of investigating four murders, not just three. Serial killers are us."

Sickened by his vitriolic speech, she said, "Well, I'm glad we stepped in and prevented you from taking yet another life. Your lack of remorse is noted and will be passed on to the CPS. Good luck in court. You're going to need it."

He grinned broadly as Craig and Barry led him out of the barn.

Sara rushed to Gordon Abbott's side. "Do you need an ambulance?"

"No, don't bother. He's broken my leg. If someone can give me a lift to the hospital?"

"I'll drop you off myself. First things first, I think we should call your wife, let her know that you're safe."

He nodded and smiled. "I'm thankful that you showed up when you did, Inspector. I'll be forever in your debt."

"We'll need a statement from you and your wife in the near future." She handed him her phone, and he rang his wife. Sara drifted away from him to give them some privacy. She approached the barn door and inhaled a lungful of fresh air.

Carla joined her, looking concerned. "Are you all right? He's not dead, is he?"

"No, I'm just catching a breather. I've given him some space to call his wife. He's refused an ambulance. I've told him we'll drop him off at the hospital. I'm presuming he'll get his wife to pick him up from there."

"What a relief, makes sense. Hey, we did well in the end. At least we saved his life."

"For which he's extremely grateful. We'll drop him off at A and E and then get the interviews underway at the station."

"I'm assuming you'll want to interview the mother first; she'll be the one more likely to talk. I bet you twenty quid the son goes down the 'no comment' route."

"I'd be foolish to take you up on that. I think it's a no-brainer."

They watched the two cars, carrying the killers, leave.

"I'll see if he's ready to go now," Sara said.

"I'll lend a hand. It won't be easy getting him to his feet on your own."

"Here's the key to my car. Maybe you should collect it. It'll be easier for all concerned."

Carla took the keys and trotted off down the lane.

Sara returned to see if Abbott had finished his call. "All done?"

"Yes, she was relieved to hear I was all right. I didn't tell her about my leg. I didn't want her driving to the hospital while upset. I told her you had insisted I get checked over before I'm allowed to go home. There's a method in my madness, I promise. I know my wife of old."

"I'm sure you do. My partner is fetching the car, then we'll help you to your feet. How's the leg? Or is that the daftest question you're going to hear today?"

"Possibly. It's throbbing. I tend to mend easily, or should I say, I used to, in my younger days." He smiled, but it faded quickly. "I can't believe the Everards would have gone to such lengths to silence us. I knew they were angry about the farm, but bloody hell, to be driven to take three of my associates' lives, it's unthinkable."

"I know. Maybe there was more to it than met the eye. How well do you know them?"

"Well enough, at least I thought I did, until today. Ben was so angry. In all fairness, his mother wasn't as furious as her son. I realised Ben was the one calling the shots and possibly manipulating his mother. But then, I'm not a detective, you are. I just wanted you to be aware of the situation."

"Thanks. I'll bear it in mind when I'm interviewing them."

Carla entered the barn. "I'm here."

"Okay, between us, we're going to get you on your feet, Gordon."

"I think I can manage on my own, ladies." He tried to pull himself up on the bale of straw beside him, but his heel slipped on the wooden floor, and he cried out in pain.

"Stop being stubborn. Carla, can you get Gordon's other arm? On the count of three. One, two, three."

It took all their strength to get him to his feet, but they

succeeded. They hooked his arms around their shoulders and helped him out to the car. The tricky part was getting him in the backseat without injuring his leg further.

"Maybe it would be easier putting him in the passenger seat instead," Carla suggested after several failed attempts.

"It might be a better option," Gordon said.

They completed the task and then drove the injured man to the hospital, where they found his wife waiting for them in the reception area.

She cried as soon as she saw him. "You lied to me. I had a feeling you were being selective about the truth."

"I needed you here in one piece. Forgive me, darling." They held hands. "We'll be fine from here, ladies. There's really no need for you to hang around here with us. You have important work to do back at the station."

"If you're sure," Sara said.

Gordon extended his hand, and Sara shook it. "I can't thank you enough for saving me."

"It's been our pleasure. Take care. We'll be in touch in the next few days regarding the statements we need from you both."

"No problem. Get today out of the way, and we'll come to the station tomorrow, if you like."

"I'll send a uniformed officer out to see you. It'll be more convenient for you."

"As you wish. Thanks again to you and your team for rescuing me."

Sara squeezed his shoulder, and she and Carla left the hospital.

Upon their return to the station, Sara began the interviews straight away, preferring to start with Natalie Everard first.

From the second Natalie eased into the chair opposite

them, with the duty solicitor sitting alongside her, the tears flowed. Unlike her son during his arrest, she was incredibly remorseful. "I'm so sorry. Everything got out of hand before we had a chance to put a stop to it. The victims didn't deserve to die. I've had nightmare after nightmare since we killed Paul Gains."

"Can you tell me what your motive was? What drove you to kill, and torture, in Parry's case, people who you considered to be friends?"

She remained quiet, shook her head, and became inconsolable. After a few minutes of Natalie sobbing, the duty solicitor, Tina Fray, suggested they call it a day.

Aware that time was getting on, Sara agreed and asked the female police officer at the back of the room to accompany Natalie back to her cell.

"Are you going to join us for the next interview with the son?" Sara asked the solicitor.

She peered at her watch. "I can only stay for about an hour. I have a dinner engagement this evening."

"We'll see if we can speed things up. I'd hate to delay you."

The door opened, and a male officer held it for Ben Everard to enter the room.

His gaze flicked between Sara, Carla, and Miss Fray. "Who's she?"

"I'm Tina Fray, the duty solicitor. Come in, Mr Everard, we've been expecting you."

He threw himself into the spare chair and folded his arms.

Carla started the recording, announced the time, and named the people who were present in the room.

Sara opened her notebook and briefly read through the questions she'd jotted down that she wanted to specifically direct to Ben rather than his mother. "Why did you target your friends in the village?"

He grinned, and Sara's stomach muscles clenched. Here it comes, 'no comment'.

But he turned her assumption on its head and said, "Because we could, and we were good at it, too, weren't we? Go on, be honest. We had you fooled there for a while. I bet you were pulling your hair out every time a new victim showed up. Go on, admit it, if you dare."

"Not at all. For your information, this is one of the quickest investigations my team has ever solved. And shall I tell you why?"

"Surprise me," he challenged, his eyes narrowing to form tiny slits.

"Because you and your mother slipped up."

"Tell me how."

"I will, but first, you need to tell me what your motive was."

He sat forward and locked gazes with her. Sara counted the seconds before he replied; she reached the number fifteen.

"They deserved to die."

"In your opinion. I'd like to know why you believed that."

His gaze dropped to his clenched fists. "Why do you think? You appear to have all the answers, Inspector. Why don't you tell me?"

Sara flipped over the page and tapped her finger on a fact that she'd circled while having her coffee before the interview. "I believe it has something to do with your father's death." She paused, waiting for him to react. "Am I right?"

He applauded her. "I'll give you that."

"I'm confused. I have access to the coroner's report, and it clearly states he died of a heart attack."

His eyes narrowed further, and there was movement going on in his mouth, as if he were chewing on the inside of his cheek.

"Is that correct?" she prompted.

Eventually, he nodded. "He'd still be here today if it wasn't for that damn Windsor."

Carla and Sara glanced at each other, the revelation coming out of the blue and not making any sense at all.

Sara returned her attention to Everard. "What does the farmer have to do with it?"

"Plenty. He's caused us no end of trouble since he bought the farm. Our lives were peaceful and without stress before he moved in."

"I still don't get it. Why target the members of the parish council?"

"Because they let us down, especially that tosser, Parry. I've got evidence that he was taking backhanders from Windsor."

The realisation suddenly dawned on Sara. She began nodding slowly as the pieces of the puzzle slotted together. "We're aware of the video you posted online, and we've also read through the notebook we found in the lounge at your home, detailing your plan for the murders. So, what you're saying is, rather than go after Windsor yourself, you thought you'd set him up. Have I got it right?"

He smiled, showing off a couple of crooked teeth at the front. "That's right, but you cops were too dumb to follow the clues."

"I dispute that, we can't be that dumb, otherwise, you wouldn't be sitting here being questioned for the murder of three people and the attempted murder of another. I believe your rationality is a bit off there. Why didn't you go after Windsor himself?"

"Because death would have been too good for him. I wanted him to spend the rest of his life in prison."

"And now your plan has massively backfired, and you and your mother are the ones heading for prison. So maybe we weren't that dumb after all." She grinned and watched the hatred develop in Everard's eyes.

Suddenly, he leapt across the table. Sara had read the look in his eyes and was prepared for the attack. She jumped to her feet, avoiding his outstretched arms, and her chair tipped behind. He didn't get a chance for a second attempt to grab her because the officer on guard at the back of the room pounced on him and pinned him to the floor. Carla pressed the alarm, and the desk sergeant burst through the door to assist them.

"Take him back to his cell, let him calm down, then I want him processed and arrested for the murder of Reverend Paul Gains, Victoria Holt and Councillor Alex Parry, and for the attempted murder of Gordon Abbott. Do the same with his mother, Natalie Everard."

Between them, Jeff and the uniformed officer pulled Everard to his feet. Sara could hear him shouting, causing mayhem all the way down the corridor to his cell.

"Well, that was eventful," Tina Fray said.

"Sorry you had to witness that, Miss Fray. At least you got your wish about finishing early this evening."

They all laughed. Sara and Carla accompanied Miss Fray back to the reception area, where she shook hands with Sara.

"Are you all right?" Carla asked as they were walking up the stairs.

"Weary but delighted, it's all over. I'm going to ring the victims' families, let them know what's happened and then call it a day. If you guys want to finish now, you can."

"I'll hang around. Do you want me to call someone for you, ease the load on your shoulders?"

"That'd be great, thanks, partner, and then you can tell me why you've been distant throughout the investigation."

"I was being silly. One of my uncles was a vicar. It brought back memories of his death."

Sara paused on the stairs. "What happened to him?" she asked, sensing there was more to come.

"He was tortured. Someone nailed him to the cross in the church."

"What? No way. I didn't know. I'm so sorry, Carla."

"It happened years ago. The killer is behind bars. No, he's not. He's in a mental institution. He blamed my uncle for the death of his father."

"Why?"

"Because my uncle and his family were in a car crash, the man driving the other car died at the scene. The PM revealed he was drunk before he got behind the steering wheel."

"How awful." Sara hugged her partner.

"I'm okay. I thought I was over it until I saw the vicar swaying in the breeze."

"Don't bottle things up in the future."

"I won't, I promise."

EPILOGUE

The day finally arrived that neither Sara nor Mark were looking forward to—his mother's funeral. As they'd wrapped up the case, Sara suggested they surprise his father and travel a day earlier than planned. James Fisher was overwhelmed to see them when Mark used his key to let themselves in. They found him staring out of the patio doors in the kitchen, admiring the garden that had been his wife's greatest pleasure in life when she wasn't running the restaurant she owned.

"Dad?"

James swiftly turned, his hand automatically covering his chest. "God, you scared the crap out of me. I wasn't expecting you two until the morning." Tears glistened in his eyes, and they all took several steps to meet each other in the middle of the kitchen.

He hugged Sara and kissed her on the cheek.

"How are you, James?" she asked.

"I've had better days, weeks, sweetheart. You look tired. Are you all right?"

"A heavy week, nothing compared to what you must have been through."

"I can't thank you enough for all you've done. Planning out what I needed to do to arrange the funeral was a great help for me."

"Nonsense, it's what family do for each other."

He hugged Mark. "I'm so glad you could both be here with me."

"We wouldn't have it any other way, Dad. Mum meant the world to both of us."

"Why don't you two catch up while I put the kettle on and make a coffee?" Sara suggested.

"A tea would be lovely, thanks, Sara," James replied.

Mark wrapped an arm around his father's shoulder, and they left the kitchen. After preparing the mugs for their drinks, Sara opened the patio door and stepped into the garden. The security light lit up, allowing her to see the splendour of the pots and borders, even at this late time of year.

"You did a fabulous job, Liz. I hope you're looking down on us." A sudden breeze ruffled the viburnum bush ahead of her. Sara smiled, taking the movement as a sign from Mark's mother.

The kettle clicked off, and she returned to make the drinks.

They spent the next couple of hours flicking through photo albums and reminiscing. Sara wasn't bored in the slightest, listening to the wonderful memories the father and son shared. It was a privilege and honour to be included.

THE FOLLOWING DAY, dressed in their smartest black suits, the three of them followed the hearse to the crematorium. Liz had always told her husband she didn't want a sombre affair for her funeral. And as a family, they fulfilled her wishes in the music they had chosen and in the eulogies Mark and his father read out to the packed chapel.

The pub nearby hosted a wake for the fifty funeral attendees. Liz would have loved the send-off they gave her. There wasn't a dry eye at the end of the day, when Mark's dad thanked everyone for attending.

They drove home together. As expected, his father was very reflective when they arrived back at the house.

Sara insisted they should have a mini send-off of their own, and she opened the bottle of red wine she had picked up from the supermarket a few days earlier.

They raised their glasses. "To Liz, she'll always be around you, James, around us."

"I hope so, Sara, because I'm going to be lost without her. For forty years that woman was the light in my life and the air in my lungs."

Sara smiled, and Mark threw an arm around his father's shoulders.

"We did her proud today, Dad."

James nodded. "It's what she deserved, son. I can't thank you enough for being here with me today and for standing by my side for the rest of my life."

They shared a hug that brought tears to Sara's eyes. She knew that with their help, James would live a fulfilling life, even without his rock beside him.

THE END

Thank you for reading Gone... But Where?, Sara and Carla's next adventure can be found here Vanished

Have you read any of my fast-paced other crime thrillers yet? Why not try the first book in the award-winning Justice series Cruel Justice here.

OR THE FIRST book in the spin-off Justice Again series, Gone In Seconds.

WHY NOT TRY the first book in the DI Sam Cobbs series, set in the beautiful Lake District, To Die For.

PERHAPS YOU'D PREFER to try one of my other police procedural series, the DI Kayli Bright series which begins with The Missing Children.

OR MAYBE YOU'D enjoy the DI Sally Parker series set in Norfolk, Wrong Place.

OR MY GRITTY police procedural starring DI Nelson set in Manchester, Torn Apart.

OR MAYBE YOU'D like to try one of my successful psychological thrillers She's Gone, I KNOW THE TRUTH or Shattered Lives.

KEEP IN TOUCH WITH M A COMLEY

Pick up a FREE novella by signing up to my newsletter today.
https://BookHip.com/WBRTGW

BookBub
www.bookbub.com/authors/m-a-comley

Blog

http://melcomley.blogspot.com

Why not join my special Facebook group to take part in monthly giveaways.

Readers' Group

TikTok
https://www.tiktok.com/@melcomley

Printed in Dunstable, United Kingdom